"Am I your protégée?" Krista asked, her tone guarded.

At the moment, Lance wasn't in the mood for sparring with her. He wanted warmth, the lithe strength of her body, the sweetness of her touch....

"A mentor is considered a good thing, according to the business gurus," he told her.

She turned her face to his and met his gaze. "It makes the other person subordinate to the mentor."

"You want equality," he murmured.

"I want to be treated as a business associate with a mind of my own. I have ideas...and plans."

He cupped his hand under her chin, feeling the smoothness of her skin against his palm.

"You have good ideas. You're great at making plans," he agreed, unable to keep the huskiness from his voice.

Then he did a foolish thing.

He kissed her.

Dear Reader,

When I was little, a friend of my parents (she was in her eighties and planning a trip to some exotic place) told me to think of each day as an adventure. As a writer I initially discounted this advice when I thought of an orphan who has already been through some perilous times. She doesn't want adventure. Instead, she trains her keen intellect and creative nature on the business at hand. That does not include romantic wrangling with a corporate raider such as Lance Carrington! Naturally I had to find out what happens when she goes on the greatest adventure of all—that of falling in love....

Best wishes,

Laurie Paige

ACQUIRING MR. RIGHT

LAURIE PAIGE

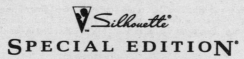

Published by Silhouette Books

America's Publisher of Contemporary Romance

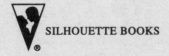

SILHOUETTE BOOKS

ISBN-13: 978-0-373-24792-9
ISBN-10:   0-373-24792-3

ACQUIRING MR. RIGHT

Visit Silhouette Books at www.eHarlequin.com

Printed in U.S.A.

Books by Laurie Paige

Silhouette Special Edition

LAURIE PAIGE

"One of the nicest things about writing romances is researching locales, careers and ideas. In the interest of authenticity, most writers will try anything…once." Along with her writing adventures, Laurie has been a NASA engineer, a past president of the Romance Writers of America, a mother and a grandmother. She was twice a Romance Writers of America RITA® Award finalist for Best Traditional Romance and has won awards from *Romantic Times BOOKclub* for Best Silhouette Special Edition and Best Silhouette, in addition to appearing on the *USA TODAY* bestseller list. Recently resettled in Northern California, Laurie is looking forward to whatever experiences her next novel will send her on.

For my pal, Alison, and the many treks through the desert near her home and to the trip we've planned down the Grand Canyon…someday.

Chapter One

Krista Aquilon parked close to the entrance of the Heymyer Home Appliances Company. The shiny red compact sedan was the first *new* auto she'd ever owned, and she was rather proud of the birthday present she'd bought for herself.

That thought usually cheered her, but not today. She unlocked the door and went into the silent building.

It was Sunday, the second day of April. The day after her birthday. Sometimes she wondered if the Fates had been laughing when they planned her birth date. She'd been an April Fool's baby, a fact that had gotten her a lot of teasing while growing up.

At any rate, she tried to keep Sundays free of work in order to maintain the illusion of a personal life, but today was an exception. The health of the company rather than her own well-being was foremost in her mind. As chief financial officer, she had a lot to worry about.

The place wasn't doing well. And all her suggestions for reviving it had been ignored, for the most part.

Pausing in the act of locking the entrance door behind her, she realized there was a red sports car under the portico at the side of the building, a space strictly reserved for James M. Heymyer, her eighty-year-old boss and a stickler for protocol.

His concept of protocol, she thought. She was more egalitarian in her views.

A reluctant smile tugged at her lips as she pictured the stunned outrage on his face at the audacity of anyone parking in his place. Not even Mason, Heymyer's son and heir, would be that bold. However, since it was Sunday, the boss wouldn't be in, so it probably didn't matter.

Returning to the original concerns that had brought her into the office, she sighed as she crossed the atrium-type lobby and went up the steps to the second floor.

All the executive offices were located on this level. "VIP Row," the other employees called it, as if the initials were a word. She'd gone from the plant production lines as a student on a work/study program during her college years to a "VIP" three years ago. After getting a business degree, she'd been promoted to accounts supervisor, then manager of the accounting department. She'd landed the head financial position last fall after earning her MBA.

At twenty-five, that could be considered quite a feat, but she was pretty sure the old man hadn't been able to get anyone else to fill the slot, which had been empty since the former CFO retired eighteen months ago.

One look at the books and anyone with a grain of sense would have run the other way, she grimly reminded her conscience, or whatever it was that wouldn't let her give the place up as a lost cause.

However, unless someone came up with a solution—and fast—Heymyer Home Appliances was gasping its last.

While the company marketed products under its own name, it also manufactured appliances for other brands. In fact, that was the bulk of their income. They had lost a major contract last week. Without it, they wouldn't have the cash flow to meet the payroll by the end of July.

In a town the size of Grand Junction, Colorado, population fifty thousand, a business failure leaving a thousand employees out of work would have a serious impact on the community. The city would lose one of its important revenue sources. The many mom-and-pop stores in town would struggle. Some might have to close. Even professionals—doctors, lawyers, bankers—would be affected.

Worst of all, families would suffer. Fear and tension caused quarrels and broken marriages. Children would be hurt. And that bothered Krista most of all. She knew how it felt to be frightened and helpless in a world that didn't seem to care.

She stopped at the top of the stairs. A light was on in the end office, the one belonging to the president and CEO. Some instinct warned her this wasn't good.

Or perhaps the boss was taking her warnings about bankruptcy seriously and had come in to study her idea to take a bold new tack.

But James Heymyer driving a red roadster? No way. So who was in his office?

As she walked down the carpeted hallway, she heard voices. Male voices. One she recognized as belonging to the boss. The low, rich timbre of the other wasn't familiar to her.

She paused at her door, listening to the tone. The depth and resonance of the voice were almost like a caress.

Krista had barely sat down and pulled up the latest balance sheet on her computer when Heymyer appeared at the door.

"James, good morning," she said warmly.

As soon as she was made a department head, she'd started calling the owner by his given name. A mental image of his eyebrows nearly flying off his forehead the first time she'd done so came to her.

But he hadn't said anything.

Too bad. She'd had her points lined up about being on equal footing with the other managers—all men, who called the big boss "James"—and being taken seriously by them.

And the owner.

"What the hell are you doing here? I didn't know you planned to come in today," he now said in accusatory tones.

"The place is usually empty on Sundays," she said, her tone level. "It's quiet, and I wanted to go over the financials before the staff meeting tomorrow."

She kept her expression pleasant and her mouth closed. He'd long since made it clear he didn't want any further ideas from her on saving the company. However, when she reported the cash flow problems tomorrow, he was going to have to face the fact that bankruptcy was looming.

A helpless anger ran through her, making it harder to hold back the recitation of all they could have done to save the business. *If* he had listened.

"I guess you may as well meet Lance today," James told her in a resigned tone.

Lance?

The guy with the sleek red car, she decided. The one who'd brought the old man to the office, an act so unusual she couldn't figure out what it might mean.

That instinctual alarm rolled through her again. She reluctantly shut down the computer and headed for the end office with James. Annoyance filled her now. She'd expected to be alone and so was dressed in faded jeans and a long-sleeved T-shirt with sneakers. No makeup.

Oh, well. It didn't make a bit of difference. In a small, home-grown company like this, everyone dressed pretty casual, even James…unless he was meeting with the bankers. Then the executives were alerted to dress the part of successful businesspeople.

They crossed the secretary's office and went into the inner sanctum, where heads sometimes rolled and shattered egos splattered the walls. She'd seen grown men nearly cry as Heymyer picked their reports apart. She'd also been on the receiving end of his sharp tongue.

She stopped in the middle of the huge office when a man, standing at one of the many windows, turned to them.

"Lance, this is the financial officer I was telling you about," James began the introduction. "Krista, this is Lance Carrington."

"How do you do?" Krista smiled politely and tried to keep the anxiety out of her expression. She had an eerie feeling about all this. Just what had James told this man about her? And why?

"Fine, thanks," the man replied. "Krista...Aquilon, isn't it?"

She nodded and, without thinking, spelled her last name as she'd had to do all her life with teachers and other officials. Most people didn't know how to translate the pronunciation—Ah-KEE-lon—into the correct spelling.

The smile widened on the handsome face. His gaze seemed warm and...and intimate, as if he knew her well.

Her insides gave a startled lurch, which interrupted her mental processes.

She stared wordlessly at the newcomer. He was dressed casually in navy slacks and a white shirt, the sleeves rolled up on his forearms. His nearly black hair had a healthy sheen, highlighted by the sunlight streaming through the window behind him, and an attractive wave in front. His eyes were gray, like winter rain, and his gaze was direct. She looked away.

"Have a seat," James told them, taking his place behind the antique desk. An odd expression flicked across his face. "Well, I guess you should be sitting here now," he said to his guest.

Puzzled, Krista glanced from James to the stranger and back.

"Tomorrow, at the staff meeting," James continued,

meeting her eyes with a harsh scowl on his face, "I'll be announcing the sale of the company to Lance."

The news hit her like a sneaky punch to the head, leaving her reeling with a thousand questions. Like times in the past when her future had been rearranged without her consent, she felt the old familiar uncertainty caused by life's nasty little tricks.

But she wasn't a child any longer. Instead of fear, anger bubbled beneath her self-control at this announcement.

"To CCS, actually," the visitor explained, his gaze piercing, as if he could see right into her brain and knew all the confused, conflicting emotions whirling there.

The man's name rang a bell. Lance Carrington. Corporate raider. Facts unfurled in her mind with the speed of light.

There had been an interview with him in a financial magazine last year. His company, CCS—which stood for Computer Control Systems—was actually a holding pen for all the shares of other companies he'd raided over the years.

Under the CCS banner, he bought ailing businesses, took them apart, remade them, then sold or merged the remains into his other operations.

She didn't need a magnifying glass to read the writing on the wall: it was the end of Heymyer Home Appliances.

A thousand employees out of work. Frightened families with no means of support. All because of one stubborn old man and his damned indifference.

And there was her own spent labor. Days and nights poring over books and ledgers, researching, then arguing for changes, trying to fix things, anything to bring the company out of its long, slow decline.

All that work. All for nothing.

White-hot anger speared through her as she stared into gray eyes as emotionless as a mountain lake in winter.

She tore her gaze away and looked her boss—her former boss—in the eye. "The entire plant was sold?"

"Yes."

His tone was aggressive, informing her she had no part in the decision. The company was private and entirely owned by James, his wife and their son. While she wasn't on the governing board, she was the chief financial officer. She should have been included in the discussion.

"Your wife and son agreed?"

"They had no choice," the old man said. He slumped into the chief executive chair, which to her seemed a mockery of the position.

"I seem to have missed the meeting when this was decided," she said, unable to keep the frost out of her voice.

"It was by teleconference. Weekend before last,"

he added when she continued to frown at him without saying anything.

Krista quickly reviewed her recent schedule. She'd visited her family back in Idaho that weekend. It was the one and only vacation she'd taken in months, and had coincided with the special dedication of a sculpture done by her beloved uncle Jeff, which had been part of a city-wide celebration of spring and renewal.

Renewal. How ironic. And how convenient that she'd been out of town during that momentous meeting. With James holding the controlling shares, his wife and son would have had to go along with him.

"Do you know who he is?" she demanded, speaking in a very soft, very controlled tone. "Do you realize what you've done?" Unable to sit still, she strode to the window and spun toward the men, her hair lashing the side of her face at the abruptness of the move.

"I did what I had to do," the older man told her. His lined face now held only weariness.

She felt his grief, recognized the anger and despair in his eyes. Pity slowly supplanted the anger. She knew how it felt to be forced into unwanted circumstances by an unchangeable fate. Oh, yes, she knew…

Except he *could* have changed it, some part of her that was harder and less forgiving chimed in.

If the ideas she'd come up with had been implemented a year ago, things might have been different.

For all his protests about saving the company, she realized James was perhaps too tired or his vision too narrow to picture a different future.

Young blood. That's what was needed. Renewal.

She studied Lance Carrington carefully. He was young, mid-thirties probably.

But renewal wouldn't happen with a corporate raider. That type was only interested in a quick profit, not the long-term investment it would take to turn things around.

She met his level perusal with one of her own and got the feeling he was amused by the situation.

Okay, it was a done deal. She'd learned a long time ago that people had to move on when life dealt them a new hand. A thousand people would have to adjust. Including her.

"You know, James," the corporate raider said, his eyes narrowed as if he were thinking aloud, "Krista is an officer of the company. She can introduce me to the staff in the morning, if you prefer. That way, you wouldn't have to come in," he added, his gaze on her again.

"That's a great idea," James said, obviously relieved to be let off the hook.

Coward, Krista thought. When the going got tough, a lot of supposedly tough people got going as fast as their feet would carry them…in the opposite direction.

Well, surprise, surprise. This was one time when

she wasn't going to stay and try to pick up the pieces. Neither was she going to be the flunky who assured the employees, people she'd worked with for over six years, that everything was going to be fine when she knew it wasn't.

"So I'm going to be stuck introducing the man who's going to close down the plant and cost us all our jobs?" she inquired in a mockingly amused manner.

She studied each of them for a long moment to let the question sink in.

"No, thanks." She headed for the door. "I quit."

"Be back in a minute," Lance said, then strode down the corridor just in time to see the top of the CFO's head disappear down the stairs. He followed, taking the steps two at a time, and caught up with her at the front door.

She muttered a distinct one-word imprecation while trying to get the key into the lock. Her hand was trembling, not much, but enough to make her awkward. The fury still gleamed in her eyes.

"Hold on," he said.

She didn't have to tilt her head upward very much to give the impression she could stare him down. She was a tall woman, probably five-nine to his six-one. Even in jeans and a T-shirt, she had a kind of grace and elegance he found very attractive.

When she added a ferocious frown to the silent

treatment, he stopped the wayward thoughts and suppressed a smile. Now wasn't the time. Okay, he could concede she had a right to be angry, at least from her point of view.

From his, it was a different matter. Based on all the company records he'd read during the two months prior to entering negotiations to buy the firm, he'd been prepared to be impressed upon meeting the financial guru. That was an understatement.

While he'd known about the clarity of her thinking, the ideas she'd developed and the sheer business acumen for one of her age and experience, what he hadn't known, hadn't even considered, was the physical package that went with the brilliant mind.

That sweep of hair, those big brown eyes, the tawny skin with the natural blush across the high cheekbones—

She gave a soft snort of exasperation, turned the key in the lock and sailed out the door before he'd quite got his thoughts in order.

Bringing himself back to the situation at hand, Lance hurried to catch up with her as she made a beeline toward her car.

"I want to explain something to you."

"Explain away," she invited airily without slowing her pace. As they neared the vehicle, she clicked the button on her key chain. The doors unlocked.

She turned to him when she stopped beside the

modest car, the bright April sunlight filling her face until she seemed to glow from within. Her eyes were dark at the outer edges, he saw, but golden around the pupil. Her hair was a very dark brown, nearly black in hue. It lay against her shoulders in a smooth, shiny curtain.

He found he wanted to touch it. To touch her.

"What is it?" she demanded, interrupting the images running through his mind.

"No one's going to lose his or her job," he said, surprised and a little irritated at the persistent track of his wandering thoughts.

"Right."

This was said with such sarcasm, it made him smile. Her lips whitened as she pressed them together, probably to hold in other, more scathing words.

"It's true. If the employees are capable and reliable," he added, qualifying the statement, "then they'll have nothing to fear."

"For how long?" She hooked her hair behind one ear and tilted her head to the side as she perused him. "How long until you sell the profitable operations and close down the rest, selling off the plant and equipment to the highest bidder so that there's nothing left of Heymyer Home Appliances? Except the name, which you can also sell since it has an established reputation in the market."

"There are no plans to do that." Although he did have plans concerning the place, he wouldn't discuss those with her until he was sure she was on board. She had to agree to stay and work with *him* first of all.

"Fine. I'm sure you'll make the place a huge success."

"As you've tried to do for the past three years," he added softly.

She stiffened as resentment flared in her eyes and was gone, then she stared at him, her face a careful blank. "Not me," she denied. "I just kept the books."

The ensuing silence hummed like busy bees around them as they sized each other up. Around them, the desert bloomed from recent spring rains, filling the air with the pleasing aroma of sage and cedar and hidden woodland flowers along the riverbanks. The world seemed fresh and new. From the company's vantage point near the forks of the Colorado and Gunnison rivers, he could hear the muted roar of the merging water. It added a pleasing ambiance to a day that had started off triumphant and now was merely trying.

Heymyer had been on target when he'd said the CFO was headstrong.

Lance was willing to let her have her way…to a certain extent, the limits being that she cooperated rather than hindered his efforts to come out of this deal with a viable, profitable company.

"I expect to see you in the office at eight in the morning," he told her, his tone harder.

"Sorry, but I no longer work here." She opened the car door, nearly striking him in the chest.

He sidestepped, then moved forward so she couldn't close it. The heat from their bodies radiated over each other, making him once more aware of her in a physical way.

He sensed the merging of their individual energies and felt it as a mighty force, like the joining of the two rivers. "I don't accept your resignation."

The eyelashes swept up and he caught the golden sparkle as anger flashed anew. She was all fire and brilliance, he mused, like a perfectly cut gem. He wanted to capture that fire, to claim that brilliance.

For the benefit of CCS, of course.

When he was involved with business, no other aspects of life entered into it. Passion was part of his personal time and not on his corporate agenda.

However, his body reacted with a sudden, sharp and unexplained need that surprised him. The hunger held passion, yes, and other things mixed in with it, things he couldn't name, things that ignited from the sparks thrown off by this very bright, very alluring woman.

Her gaze didn't waver. "You can't force me to stay."

"I know," he said quietly. "I'm asking you to."

That caused her to blink. "No."

He shrugged and stepped back one pace as she slid into the driver's seat of the wagon. "So it was a lie."

"What was?" Her manner was wary.

"All your concern about the place closing and people losing their jobs."

"No. It wasn't. I do care."

"Then stay and help me make it a successful operation. James said you had plenty of ideas. I want to hear them."

She laughed, a sudden, sexy sound that had his insides clenching up. "He called them dingbat notions. Still want to hear them?"

"Yeah." He stuck his hands in his pockets and rocked back on his heels as he smiled at her, one cohort to another. "I believe we can turn this company around and make it one of the best in the country. How does that sound to a CFO with bulldog tenacity, or so James warned me, and lots of ideas?"

Wariness returned. "Great. If you mean it."

"I do." He held out his hand. "Deal?"

She held both hands up, palms out as if to hold him off. "What deal?"

"You'll stay for a minimum of six months, and work with me to put the company back on track."

"As CFO?"

"Maybe," he answered.

She put the car key in the ignition. "I don't play games," she said coldly.

"Sorry. Truly," he added at the dismissive glance. "I'm serious. You're a valuable asset to the company, but I'm not sure yet just what the new job titles will be. For now, you're still the CFO. So, will you come aboard?"

He found himself anxious for her reply. He was banking on her already considerable investment of time and energy in the company, and also her curiosity about him and the future, to convince her to stay. He knew the moment she decided in his favor by the slight smile that curved her lips, displaying two barely discernible dimples in her cheeks.

"Yes. I will." She held out a hand. "Six months...and then we'll see," she added.

Electricity flowed up his arm as they shook on the agreement. Six months, he thought as he watched her drive off. A lot could happen in six months. A working team could be built. A company could be turned around. An attraction—any attraction—would have to be stamped out.

Chapter Two

Krista considered her wardrobe for several minutes on Monday morning before selecting black slacks, a blue cotton sweater and a matching bouclé jacket.

She applied her makeup carefully and left her hair down, then pulled on ankle boots with one-and-a-half-inch heels. She was as ready as she'd ever be.

Driving from her town house apartment complex to the office, she marveled that the day could look so normal. The sun was shining, no clouds marred the sky and the traffic flowed without any delays. To her mind, there should be thunder and lightning to herald the momentous event—the takeover of the company by a man who had no ties to the community, no motivation for its success except profit.

Or maybe the change was momentous only to her, she mused sardonically.

Memories of other changes in her life flooded into her mind. When she was nine, her mom and stepfather had divorced. On a snowy night that same winter he'd died in a car crash. Six months later her mom had gotten in the way of a stray bullet when one angry neighbor shot another and had also died. As a runaway from foster care, her tenth year had been a period of uncertainty, always looking over her shoulder, never knowing what was going to happen next and feeling that life was as tenuous as a cobweb.

While she couldn't exactly define the reasons, she felt somewhat like that now—unsure and anxious about the future.

She was no longer that child, she grimly reminded herself as she pulled into the parking lot at the plant. No one could push her around. And no corporate raider was going to intimidate her.

Nodding her head decisively, she parked in her usual place under the shade of the oak tree in the far back corner of the large lot and strode to the office.

Upstairs, VIP Row was unusually quiet.

When Krista entered the CFO office suite, her secretary was hanging up her jacket. "Good morning, Tiff."

Krista had inherited the secretary from the last CFO. After a rocky start, Tiffany Adams—late forties, divorced, one grown son—had transferred her loyalty to the new boss and now they worked together as a close-knit team.

Tiff nodded toward the end office. "Something's going on," she said in a low, ominous manner.

"I know." Krista checked the wall clock. She had twenty minutes before the staff meeting. "I'm going to introduce the new owner to the managers this morning."

"New owner!" the other woman said in a shocked whisper.

"Shh," Krista warned, nodding toward the open door. "I'll tell you all about it after the meeting." She went into her office.

Frowning, she realized she'd forgotten to lock her desk after the shock of meeting Lance Carrington yesterday. She gathered the financial reports, the cash flow estimates and projected earnings before exiting through the private door that connected the conference room to her office.

The elegant meeting space with its carved walnut table and twelve executive chairs separated her suite from that of the chief executive's. Coffee, she noted, was brewing in the silver urn on the credenza.

She wondered if Thea, the CEO's secretary, was in yet and if James had warned her of the pending changes. The woman was in her sixties and had worked there for more than forty years. Totally loyal to the big boss, she'd watched out for his interests like a pit bull.

A light was on inside the end office and Krista could see the outline of a person moving about in there through the frosted glass of the adjoining door.

She stopped in the act of placing copies of her reports at each manager's seat and stared at the masculine figure who seemed to alternate between pacing and staring out the windows at the scenery.

Was Carrington…Lance, she corrected…nervous about the meeting?

Hmm, she couldn't picture that. He was hard-edged and confident. Besides, he held all the winning cards in this venture, whatever it was to him.

While she was still staring at the indistinct figure through the glass, the door swung inward. He filled the opening like the hero in a movie close-up, backlit by the windows behind him and appearing bigger than life.

"Good morning," he said, coming into the conference room and closing the door.

The odd impressions—that of him being nervous or being a super screen hero—fled. He was once more just a man, handsome and dynamic, yes, but not overpowering.

Well, not totally overpowering.

"Good morning." She finished her task, then hesitated, not sure where she should sit.

"Here's where you sit," Lance said, as if reading her mind. He pulled out the chair at one end of the table.

That was Mason's place, when he deigned to be present, but she didn't say anything. She supposed, like his father, he was now out of the company.

Lance pulled the chair back for her as she approached. Closer to him, she became aware of him in a whole new way.

In fact, her senses seemed keenly in tune today. First of all, he smelled really, really good. Visually, he looked cosmopolitan in a suit of medium gray with a thin navy blue stripe, a navy shirt and a silk tie of silvery gray. Looking at him almost made her dizzy. It was the oddest sensation.

Frowning at the reaction, she quickly placed her folders on the table and went to the coffee urn. He followed right behind her.

Ignoring the pastries on a silver server, she filled a china cup and returned to her seat.

The new boss also rejected the rich Danish rolls and muffins. Taking his cup, he sat at the opposite end of the table. "Nice day," he said.

"Yes. The sunshine is...nice." At that brilliant start, she almost groaned aloud.

Glancing down the shining length of the conference table, she detected a gleam in his eyes. A smile swept over his face, changing him from the serious tycoon to a coconspirator in an intrigue still to be played out.

His eyes no longer seemed wintry to her as they had yesterday. Instead they were cordial.

Inviting.

Intimate.

The warmth in those depths reached inside her, making her aware of things she hadn't considered in a long time…a sense of security, the way she'd felt as a teenager growing up in Uncle Jeff's home. And something more…

She shook her head to rid herself of the new sensation. While James had listened when she explained the financial situation, he had been impatient with her ideas for change. Maybe this new CEO would think her suggestions brilliant and let her try some of them.

The absurdity of that idea hit her. A corporate raider, who'd probably leveraged the buyout so that the company was now also in debt up to its neck, letting her have her way?

She forced her gaze to the documents she'd prepared while her heart pounded out a salsa beat in her ears. The arrival of the eight managers helped still the sudden, unexplained tumult.

From their quick glances at Lance, then her, she knew they'd already heard about the new man in the boss's office and knew something unusual was up. Following ritual, they filled their coffee cups and took their seats. They, too, ignored the treats that were usually a big hit and gone before the meeting was over.

"Good morning," she said with a calm smile, standing and taking charge as Lance shot her a glance down the table that told her to do so.

Right. She was to introduce him. Which made her feel rather like some kind of Judas to the old order of things.

"By now, each of you are aware of changes in the company, so I won't keep you in suspense."

She introduced Lance as the head of CCS and announced the sale of Heymyer to the other company. Varying degrees of shock and alarm flashed into the men's faces and were gone. They could have been statues, they sat so still.

Starting on Lance's right, she introduced the six general managers, who had charge of specific production areas, and the two marketing managers, who reported to the vice president, which had been Mason up until yesterday.

Krista glanced at the two empty chairs. James's secretary normally sat on his left side and took notes at the meetings. Had Lance told her she wasn't needed today? And was Mason still the VP? She could see similar questions in the men's eyes.

Changes. Sometimes they were for the good. If Lance meant what he'd said about not closing the place, then all would be well. Maybe.

"I'll turn the meeting over to our new CEO," she finished and sat down.

All eyes turned to the other end of the table.

"Acting CEO," he said, still seated, his manner casual. "Heymyer will be a subsidiary of CCS, the same as Applied Controls."

Krista recalled the original computer control company had been spun off CCS as its own corporate entity, its shares retained by the parent company, and renamed.

"As with our other companies, Heymyer will have its own CEO. First of all, no changes are imminent. Rumors will abound, but each of you should assure your employees that there are no plans to close the plant. The work schedule will continue as usual. I know the change of ownership will be unsettling to a degree, but I don't expect production to drop during the transition," he told them.

His manner was as reassuring as his statements, which were delivered in a confident, decisive tone. Whatever had caused him to pace his office earlier like a restless tiger was well hidden. Or put out of his mind altogether.

She tended to do that—concentrate so fiercely on one thing that everything else disappeared— much to the annoyance of some men she'd dated. Her one serious relationship had ended in failure. Truth was, she wasn't sure what men wanted, but *she* wanted someone who really meant forever when he spoke of love.

Her glance went to the new owner. Not someone like him, she quickly asserted, as if he'd been put forward as an example. By nature, a raider was a hit-and-run specialist.

"For the foreseeable future," Lance was saying, "there will be lots of meetings between this team and the CCS board and executive staff while we work out the integration of goals and procedures."

And then, she thought, his staff will know the company inside out and can dispense with us.

She studied the eight managers, all listening with serious expressions on their faces. Six had been there long enough to retire with full pensions. The other two, one in his late forties, the other in his mid-fifties, hadn't. Where would they go?

For the next three hours, Lance asked for reports from each person at the table. When she explained the cash flow problems resulting from the lost contract, she knew by his questions and the keen intelligence in his eyes that he understood the situation at once. Also that James hadn't mentioned this latest bit of news.

"They canceled the order the day before the breach-of-contract penalties kicked in?" he asked.

Understanding flashed between them as they exchanged glances. She would share her concerns about that contract when they were alone.

Shortly after eleven, the new boss seemed satisfied with the reports. "I have one other announcement," he said, his gaze on her.

A startled throb jolted to life inside her.

"Krista, will you come here, please?"

Her first thought was that he was going to fire her, right there in front of everyone. The next was that he wouldn't do a thing like that. He'd asked her to stay six months, and they'd shook on it. He was too much the smart businessman to renege on a deal or shake up the managers in that way.

She rose and walked to the other end of the table, eight pairs of eyes burning holes in her head the whole way. If the men were half as confused by this request as she was, then they were all in for a surprise.

When she stood beside Lance, he smiled that megawatt smile that changed him to movie star handsome. It was a total contrast to the serious, probing manner exhibited during the long meeting.

She smiled back with a lot more confidence than she felt. She didn't like the unexpected, and she felt she was in for more aftershocks from him.

He laid a hand on her shoulder. Krista felt the heat burning into her flesh. It spread along her arm, her back, down into the innermost parts of her. Taken aback, she shifted away. The fingers tightened, just a fraction, just enough to hold her.

"While I'll be the acting CEO at present, Krista will be the Chief Operating Officer in addition to her other duties," he said. "She'll handle all day-to-day decisions and you'll report to her as of now."

For the second time in two days, she was taken completely off guard.

Lance glanced at Krista after he parked at the Rosevale Grand Inn. When he'd told her he'd arranged lunch for them at the inn so they wouldn't be interrupted while they talked, she'd agreed readily enough. However, like the elderly secretary who guarded the CEO's door, she hadn't exactly been thrilled at his plans.

"This way," he said, placing a hand in the small of her back to guide her to the garden pathway that led to the terrace, now used as an extension of the restaurant. It was his favorite place to dine and think things through.

The waitress, a friendly redhead who'd joked with him during the many weekends he'd spent there of late, smiled as he went to his usual table, glanced at Krista, then gave him a mock scowl as if reprimanding him for arriving with another woman.

Krista, he saw, noted the byplay but kept any reaction to herself.

"I've been staying here almost every weekend while deciding whether to add Heymyer to our holdings, also during the negotiations." He explained the familiarity, then wondered why he had.

He rarely justified his actions and choices to anyone anymore, figuring that was his private business.

His grandfather's tyrannical voice suddenly echoed in his head. *"Just what is the reason for this* B *on your report card?"*

"What is the meaning of this speeding ticket?"

"You're taking who *to the dance? She's nobody—"*

"So was my mother," Lance had dared to say at seventeen, as he headed for the door. *"But your son still married her."*

"He was a fool," Claude Carrington had shouted after him. *"I warned him…"*

But Lance hadn't heard the rest. He'd left the hated library where his grandfather called him on the carpet at regular intervals, and he'd never looked back.

Glancing at the lovely woman across the table, he realized if he'd kowtowed to his grandfather's wishes to join his investment firm, he would never have started his own company, might never have met this woman.

Now *that* would have been a shame, as she was easily one of the most intriguing people he'd met in a long time, whether male or female.

"I looked you up on the Internet last night," she said. "There wasn't a lot of information in the financial magazines. You've only given one in-depth interview that I could find."

"That damned article," he muttered, more to himself than her. "I should never have allowed it."

"So why did you?" she asked, openly curious.

"It was for a friend. He needed to prove he had access to people the editor couldn't otherwise get. We were roommates at college so I agreed."

"An Ivy League college. Honors. Top ten percent of your class," she reiterated as if reading his accomplishments on a tickertape.

A slight shifting in that cold place that existed deep within his psyche ruffled his enjoyment of sparring with this woman who watched him as closely as he did her.

He shrugged. "My grandfather's alma mater. I had no choice."

Into his mind's eye sprang an image—that of a young woman, one who'd once been beautiful beyond compare but now looked weary and worn out.

His mother.

Sober for the first time in months, his parents had stood silently in the corridor outside the courtroom where his grandfather had just won custody of him.

His mother had stooped and looked directly into his eyes while his dad had stared stonily at his grandfather. "We'll get you back," she'd said. "Your father and I…we'll change. Everything will be all right. You'll see."

"Okay," he'd said, believing her.

"Be a good boy," she'd whispered, squeezing his shoulders. "I love you."

"I love you, too. You and Dad."

She'd hugged him and kissed him, her tears spilling all over his face, until his grandfather had pulled him away and marched him out of the courthouse.

He would never forget that day. His tenth birthday. The last time he'd seen either of his parents alive.

Lance pushed the image into the place that, as a child, he'd imagined as a cold storage locker, a place where old memories could be safely hidden.

"CEO of your own company at twenty-two," she continued. "Fortune has smiled on your every endeavor."

Returning to the present, he assumed a mockingly cheerful air. "Yeah, I'm used to getting my own way. Don't cross me. A tantrum isn't a pretty sight."

After the waitress gave them menus, his guest studied him for a minute. "I don't think you're the type for tantrums. You're much more subtle than that. Like now."

"Now?"

"You used a change in subject to distract me from further probing into your life. This morning you got exactly what you wanted, too. By having me introduce you to the managers, it sounded as if I'd checked you out and approved of the changes."

She saw more than he liked, but then he'd

already figured out how sharp she was. "So why did you let me?"

She shrugged. "My choice was walking out or sticking it out. I agreed on the latter."

"And you keep your word," he concluded.

"I try. Do you?"

Her manner was a cover, the surface amusement hiding her doubts about him. He reached across the table and laid a hand over hers for emphasis. "Always."

When he settled back in his chair, he realized he wanted to touch her, to take her up to his room—

Damn, maybe it hadn't been the most brilliant idea to bring her to the inn. This was where he spent his private hours, even if most of that time was dedicated to reading reports. Their lunch was business, part of his public persona. Those two things, the personal and the public, should never merge, in his opinion.

"Why am I now chief of operations as well as finance?" she asked, her mind obviously having no problem focusing on work and its problems.

The answer was easy. "You know the company."

"So do all the other executives, six of whom have been there thirty years or more."

The waitress placed tall glasses of raspberry iced tea on the table and told them the day's specials.

"I'll take the salmon. Mixed green salad, house dressing on the side," he ordered, impatient with the interruption.

"The same," Krista said in an identical tone.

The redhead rolled her eyes, jotted the info on her pad, took the unopened menus and left.

"Do you always order like that?" he asked.

"Like what?"

"With little thought."

She studied him as if this might be a trick question, then she shrugged. "I enjoy good food, but it isn't my reason for living."

"But work is?"

"It's a large part of most people's lives. It helps keep body and soul together, you might say."

The droll smile that touched her lips caused the slight dimples to appear. Her eyes were darker in the shade of the terrace's white-glazed glass roof and mysterious, her true thoughts hidden as she observed him.

"So, do I get a raise along with the added responsibilities?" she questioned, a challenge in the amused tone.

"Yes."

Her eyebrows went up at the flat statement.

"I believe in paying people what they're worth," he said. "I think you're going to be worth a lot. To the company." He wasn't sure if the clarifying phrase was meant for her or himself.

The interest that had begun while studying her orderly financial statements and the many memos outlining her ideas for the company had blossomed into an attraction upon meeting her yesterday. Today her professional and personal sides had combined into one very interesting package.

He wondered if she kept those two parts as separate as he did…as he usually did. He mentally frowned and forced his thoughts to Heymyer Home Appliances, which was the reason they were here.

"If you could do anything you wanted at the company," he began, "what would be the first change you would make?"

She was silent for a moment before she said, "There wouldn't be one thing. Several changes would have to work together. New product lines. New equipment. New production processes." She paused, her eyes on the tiny rosebuds in a vase on the table. The long, lovely sweep of lashes lifted as she looked at him. "New money."

"Work up a proposal. I want the business turned around in six months."

She stared at him, then a slow smile started at the corners of her mouth and ended with a sparkle in her eyes. "I can give it to you now verbatim."

During the next two hours, they went over several of her ideas. As he listened, Lance found he liked her spunk, her enthusiasm, her wide-ranging intelligence.

If the owners of the company had listened to some of her "dingbat notions," they might have saved the business from his takeover.

As far as Lance could determine, Heymyer's wife, who held the title of secretary, was in Florida visiting her mother and sister. Their thirty-nine-year-old son operated out of their New York office. He'd been the vice president and in charge of marketing. Neither had done much good for the business that furnished their living, or so it appeared to him.

From going over the company's records before making an offer, he'd concluded that only Heymyer and the CFO were avidly involved. The home appliance manufacturer needed modernizing, a fact that Krista understood well.

"New lines," she now told him in her earnest manner. "I'm thinking of a hip name, like Uptown. Anyway, the shapes would be modern. And the colors, we should go wild with the colors—jewel tones, pastels, retro shades."

Her graceful, expressive eyebrows rose as if she had her arguments down pat in case he disagreed. She drew outlines in the air as she described new items.

When she hesitated, he nodded and smiled encouragement. The new company would fit in nicely with the original one he'd acquired, with the help of a sizable inheritance from his grandmother, shortly after he'd graduated from college.

His grandfather had been furious, but Lance had made that business a success and therefore hadn't had to accept any help from his only living relative. Only a sense of duty pushed him into visiting the old tyrant a few times a year.

For a second, he drifted back in time to those months when he'd thought his parents would come for him, when he'd believed in them with all his heart and soul. But his father had run off a bridge, his blood alcohol level twice that allowed by law, two months after the custody battle. And his mother...

The pain of the moment when he'd learned of her death swept over him. She'd died of pneumonia that winter, alone and forgotten by everyone but him.

From that day forward, he'd kept his feelings under wraps. He'd loved his grandmother, a gentle woman who'd tended her house and gardens with quiet joy, but he'd never let himself become dependent on anyone again—

God, he didn't know why those old memories had returned to haunt him at this late date. At thirty-four, with nearly thirteen years' experience behind him, he'd taken five failing companies under the CCS banner and made them into viable projects. He would do the same with this one.

None of the other five had been as interesting as this one promised to be, though. Perhaps because of the CFO and her brilliant mind and very feminine allure?

James had thought she should stick to balance sheets and leave the ideas to him. "She wants to put computers in toasters, for God's sake," the old man had said, shaking his head. He'd thought her ideas foolish because she'd wanted to make the appliances more versatile, to put computer chips in them to control the temperatures and cook times and make it possible to add features the old owner had never dreamed of.

Lance let his gaze drift over her as he listened, her lovely face filled with enthusiasm and energy. He liked her ideas and the way she challenged him, making him see the possibilities through her eyes.

Most of all, he liked being surprised by those little dimples that appeared when she smiled….

Chapter Three

Krista arrived at work thirty minutes later than normal, thanks to a flat tire. The low-slung red sports car was already in the CEO spot. Her heart thumped like a mad drummer, which quite annoyed her as she crossed the parking lot.

She halted with one foot on the sidewalk in front of the entrance. A sign was attached to a post supporting the cover over the red car. It had her name on it.

Frowning, she changed direction and went to the covered parking area. While there was space for two vehicles under the portico, no one had dared challenge James's exclusive right to the middle of the spot. Lance had left plenty of room for another car.

Disgruntled at yet another change, she marched into the building and up the stairs. Her secretary gave her a warning glance when she arrived at the door of the CFO suite.

"Good morning, Tiff. Is something up that I should know about?" she asked, pausing by the other's desk.

"Mason came in about fifteen minutes ago and headed straight for the big office."

Krista was taken aback by this information. Mason in town was a surprise, and his being at the office was a shock, especially in light of the new ownership. "Trouble?"

Tiff shrugged. "Mason raised his voice once, but since then I haven't heard anything."

Krista nodded and continued into her office. After storing her purse in the credenza, she stopped in front of an ornate wall mirror and studied her reflection.

A tiny frown of tension was evident in two little lines between her eyes. She forced the muscles to relax.

This morning she wore one of her power suits, as Uncle Jeff's wife Caileen called them. As a Family Services counselor, her aunt—step-aunt, actually, since Jeff Aquilon had been a brother to Krista's and Tony's stepfather—had helped her select clothing for the business image she'd wanted to project when she'd had to do a senior presentation in college.

Deciding against all black for her first day as the COO, she'd chosen black slacks with a gray pin-stripe. The pinstripe had a touch of red running through it. The tailored blouse was also black, but the suit jacket was a buttery soft leather in brilliant power red.

She looked, she thought, like a woman who knew what she was doing, who knew where she was going—like a woman who was used to taking charge.

Fortunately, only *she* knew her knees were knocking.

Her intercom buzzed. When she answered, Tiff told her she was wanted in the CEO's office.

Going into the corridor, she reflected that James had always opened the conference room door and bellowed her name so that it could be heard clear out to the parking lot. A polite request through the secretary was another change, one for the better, in her opinion. She hated yelling of any kind.

Before she reached the end office, she came face-to-face with Mason, who was leaving it. "Hello, Mason," she said in a friendly fashion.

He stopped in front of her, his smile more of a sneer than a greeting. "My, you certainly move fast when you put your mind to it, don't you?"

She tried to figure out just what his remark meant. When she'd first been promoted to head of the accounting department, the heir-apparent had tried to put a move on her, but she'd acted obtuse, as if she didn't catch on that he was trying to start something.

Even at twenty-two, she'd known it was bad judgment to get involved with someone who could derail her fledgling career. There was also the fact that he didn't appeal to her in any way, shape or form.

"I try," she said lightly, assuming he referred to her now being the chief operations officer and aware that all around them others were straining their ears to hear what was being said between them. "I wasn't sure you would be with us anymore."

"Where did you think I would be?" he demanded in a definite snarl.

"I thought you might decide to retire and live the life of a rich playboy," she told him, knowing he liked to imagine himself as a jet-setter.

"Not with my father controlling the purse strings," he said, anger overriding the earlier sarcasm. "And now, you're the one in charge. Maybe the new CEO will let you try some of your ideas."

His tone implied he shared his father's views of her notions. "I'll keep my fingers crossed," she said calmly.

He snorted and walked away whistling "Hail to the Chief."

At times she would really like to give him a good smack across the mouth, she acknowledged, going into Thea's office. "I understand Mr. Carrington wants to see me."

Without answering, the secretary pushed the button on her phone set. "Krista Aquilon is here."

"Ask her to come in, please," Lance said politely.

Thea nodded at Krista.

As far as Krista could remember, Thea had managed to never call her by her title or even Ms. Aquilon, as if this was beneath her lofty position. Strange woman. Krista went into the inner office.

Lance rose and came to her, hand out. Krista shook hands with him, more than a little wary. Even so, she wasn't quite prepared for the jolt of electricity that rushed up her arm and to all parts of her body.

Gray eyes flicked over her. "You look stunning this morning," he said with an approving nod.

"Actually I was going for 'person-in-charge' rather than stunning," she told him. "I blew it, huh?"

"You look like a person of immense authority," he assured her. There was laughter in his eyes. "Coffee? I just made some—apparently Thea doesn't do coffee—and it's good, if I do say so."

"Please, with one sugar." She smiled when he did, a real smile, and felt some of the tension drain out of her shoulders as she took her usual chair at the side of the big desk. "I met Mason in the hall. For some reason, I assumed he would no longer be with the company."

Lance settled behind the desk. They sipped the excellent brew in silence for a few seconds. "Did he give you any trouble?"

"Not really. He may have been a tad disappointed that he wasn't named the COO."

The new boss shrugged. "Then he should have shown some real interest in the company at some time during the past twenty years. If he gives you any problems, fire him."

Krista nearly choked on her coffee.

Lance continued. "I felt like doing that this morning when he walked in here unannounced. He was supposed to have been here yesterday for the staff meeting."

"He has a tendency to be late," she explained. "Or not show up at all. I guess he thought he could continue his old ways. My secretary said she heard him raise his voice. If he was insubordinate, why didn't you tell him to clear out?" The question was pure curiosity on her part.

"I told Heymyer I'd give everyone who wanted it a chance to stay on." Lance's dark eyebrows rose slightly. "You're the boss. You say who stays and who doesn't. If Mason doesn't work out, then he goes. Although I wouldn't toss anybody out on the first day," he offered as a suggestion. "It's unsettling for the other employees."

"Mason's the vice president—"

Lance shook his head. "The Heymyer officers are gone. You and I are the big bosses now."

She did a mental double take on that idea. "So what's his title?"

"Whatever you decide." The winter-gray eyes bored right into her. "It's your job to run the company, so that's your call. I will need an organizational chart as soon as you can get one done so my people will know who's who."

After she'd absorbed Lance's information, she asked, unable to keep the facetious tone completely under wraps, "And what will you be doing while I'm drawing up charts, checking production runs and making sure the company is running smoothly?"

"Envisioning the big picture, coming up with clever ways to integrate the operations and devising strategies to make it all mesh like clockwork."

His grin was…sardonic? Definitely.

"Well," she said, "that explains the division of labor. I'm so glad we had this chat."

"You have a smart mouth, but that's okay. I like a woman who speaks her mind."

"Good, because I have a couple of hundred questions."

For the next hour, they discussed the changes that would be necessary to save the business. It was obvious he'd had experience in smoothly melding new enterprises into CCS's operations. Krista tried not to look too naively impressed by his acumen.

"We might move some parts of production to another location," he told her, his eyes on the middle distance as if he could see those parts being transferred already.

"You said you weren't shutting down here," she reminded him with a fierce frown. "You said no one would lose their jobs, that we're going to put the company back on track. That's why I agreed to stay."

"I'm not talking about shutting down, but things aren't going to stay exactly the same. That's why the company was going downhill—it was static."

He held her gaze until she was forced to acknowledge the truth in his words. She sighed. "I know. Sorry. I'll pull in my claws."

He leaned toward her. "Sometimes claws are useful." He lifted her left hand. Her nails were short and buffed to a shine rather than polished. "With these, I don't think I have anything to worry about."

Her skin burned everywhere he touched her. Maybe he didn't have anything to worry about, but maybe she did. Shaking off the sensation, she continued their planning session.

"One other thing," she said some time later, preparing to leave. "Someone put up a sign with my name on it in a parking space next to your car. Who authorized it?"

"I did."

"Have it taken down. I already have a space I like."

"You're the COO. Don't you think you're entitled to a few perks?"

She was aware of his keen gaze on her as if she were some newly discovered pest under study. "Not that kind. It irritated me when I worked on the production line for the VIPs to assume they had more rights than anyone else. Even Mason, who was rarely here, had a reserved space."

"So where are the signs now?"

She grinned. "When I became CFO, I told the executive staff there wasn't money in the budget to replace the old signs when they needed repair. James agreed. After that, parking near the door was a perk only to those who got here early. It greatly improved the timeliness of the staff's arrival."

When he chuckled, she again found herself spellbound by the sound.

"What time do you usually come in?" he asked.

"Seven-thirty or thereabouts. I had a flat this morning, picked up a nail in a brand-new tire. There's a lot of construction going on in my neighborhood."

"Who changed the tire?"

"I did. My uncle says people need to be self-sufficient regarding minor emergencies such as flats. He taught us basic car maintenance and simple household repairs."

"Smart man." He paused, then added, "James said your mother died when you were a child."

She heard the slight upward inflection and had to decide how much she wanted him to know about her personal life. "Shortly after I turned ten."

"So you went to live with an uncle?"

Krista felt the familiar tightening inside, the shutting down of emotion when someone delved into her life. "Actually he was my stepfather's brother. He took me and my brother Tony in as well as Jeremy, his nephew. Then Social Services found out and moved me and Tony to a foster home. They said the four of us couldn't share a two-bedroom home. I slept on the sofa while Jeremy and Tony shared the spare room. At the foster home, Tony and I had our own rooms."

"It wasn't a happy experience," Lance concluded, his expression becoming grim, as if he could see the unhappiness of those children.

Unwanted memories flooded her mind. She'd broken a plate at dinner one night. Her foster father had beaten her with his belt. She'd stared into the distance and imagined escaping, running to her mother. At one point she'd felt moisture on her legs and trembled with fear, not knowing what the man would do if she'd wet her pants. But it had been blood running down her legs into her socks.

That's when Tony had sneaked out into the night and gone to their step-cousin for help.

Not wanting to disclose any emotion that those keen gray eyes would surely detect, she went to the window and gazed out at the desert land. "The foster father beat us, so we ran away with Jeremy. He was seventeen. We sort of lived off the land that summer. In the winter, Jeremy got a job at a grocery and we lived in an abandoned gas station that had had living quarters on the second floor."

"How long did you live like that?" Lance asked, his voice fathoms deep with a stillness at its center that she found oddly comforting. His reflection appeared in the windowpane next to hers. His heat swept over her, all the way to the hidden place inside.

"We were caught the following summer on a ranch. The family there went to bat for us and we were returned to our uncle, Jeff Aquilon. He became our legal guardian, and we lived happily ever after." She cast Lance a saucy grin to show him she was still living that good life.

His manner was thoughtful, as if he was connecting all the dots while he studied her. "You and your brother took your guardian's name?"

"Well, he made it legal, but our mother started using Aquilon for all of us when she married his older brother." Anticipating the next question of his very logical mind, she added, "My father walked out when I was a baby and Tony was three, so it's the only name he or I have ever known."

"I see. It must have been difficult, hiding out from the authorities all that time."

She carefully held all the old emotion in check while planting a smile on her face. "Nah, that was the fun part. The hard part was getting up the courage to run away."

"But you did it."

"Because of Jeremy. He's the one who figured out what to do. He took care of us, but he didn't have to. He wasn't kin to us by blood or legal ties. When his father, the oldest Aquilon brother, died, Jeremy came to live with us. About six months after my mother and stepfather divorced, my stepfather died in an auto accident, so Mom told Jeremy to come back to us. Jeff, the youngest of the three brothers, had been in the hospital at that time."

Silence surrounded them like a blanket. Krista felt as if she couldn't breathe, as if she were being smothered as the past pushed past her defenses and closed in on her.

Then a big, warm hand touched the back of her neck. Strong fingers massaged the tense muscles in her shoulders.

"I'm sorry," he said. "I'm sorry I made you remember."

The gentleness of his touch, the sympathy she sensed in him, caused her eyes to burn. But she'd learned long ago that tears didn't help. She managed to shake her head as if it didn't matter, to make herself not care. "Everything came out okay. Uncle Jeff got a bigger house, so that satisfied the family services people. When he married Caileen, who was the new counselor from the county welfare office, we became one big happy family. Caileen had a daughter, Zia, so I got a big sister out of the deal. That was nice."

"Ten years old," he murmured. "That's an impressionable age. Things happen that can never be forgotten."

His hand glided down her back, stopped at her waist. A need to lean into him, to feel his strength as well as his heat, alarmed her. It was time to end this conversation.

"Well, you don't forget," she admitted, stepping away from him, "but you move on." She glanced at her watch. "Speaking of which, I'd better get those organizational charts done, then I have some ideas to run by two of the production managers about merging their lines."

To her surprise, laughter erupted from him.

"Go for it," he said.

Later, in her own office while waiting for a new spreadsheet to come up on her computer, she studied her hands. There was the faintest tremor in them.

In helping her practice for her presentation, her aunt Caileen had told her to act calm and assured in uncertain situations and it would follow that she would become calm and assured. With Lance Carrington, Krista wasn't sure that would work. Something about him reached right down into her inner equilibrium and shook its moorings.

"What is going on over there?" Marlyn asked on Thursday when Krista met her for a quick lunch.

Krista smiled as her best friend's expression mirrored the shock of other residents upon learning about the company changes. "Heymyer sold us out without a word."

It was through Marlyn, whom she'd met in her freshman year at college, that she'd gotten the job with Heymyer Home Appliances. She and Marlyn had both used the work/study program to pay their way through school. They'd shared apartments, clothes and books during those years of work, study and counting pennies.

"And the new guy wants you to stay on?"

"Right."

"I thought raiders always fired all the executives and put in their own people."

"He asked me to stay six months, I guess to help with the transition. *Then* he'll fire me."

"You think?"

Krista shrugged. "We'll just have to wait and see. I'm not worried about finding a new job, but for others who've lived and worked their whole lives in this town, what happens to them?"

They both thought this over.

"His picture was in a big spread the paper did on him and CCS." Marlyn tilted her head and studied Krista. "He's only thirty-four. Rich *and* handsome."

When she waggled her brows, Krista had to laugh. "He's also strictly business."

For the briefest instant, she recalled how she'd felt when he'd stood behind her at the window, as if he'd sensed the turmoil his questions about her past had caused. His touch had been comforting.

It had also been exciting, reaching right down and stirring something inside her. A hunger, she realized, a need for touching, caressing…for fulfillment.

Enough, already, she warned her libido, or whatever it was that kept sending forbidden longings through her.

"So how are things going with your business? Does everyone in town want the famous Marlyn Reynolds of Reynolds' Interior Design to redo their homes?"

"Oh, yeah." Marlyn sighed, then smiled. "Actually things are going well with business. I just wish I could say the same about my personal life. Or lack thereof."

"Come on," Krista said, "you and Linc are solid."

"Are we?" Marlyn finished her salad and peered out the window at the mesas and rugged canyons cut by eons of wind and water erosion. "He called and said he wouldn't make it home this weekend. I told him if he didn't, not to bother coming at all, ever."

"Marlyn, you didn't!"

To Krista's consternation, tears filled the other woman's dark brown eyes. "I mean it, Krista. I've had it."

"But you've loved him since third grade. You told me it was love at first sight for both of you."

"Well, I saw him more in school than I have since we married. I'm tired of it."

"You need to talk to Linc. Surely you two can work things out."

There was a troubled silence. "I don't know," Marlyn admitted. "I'm not sure how I feel about Linc and marriage and making it as a couple anymore."

Krista couldn't conceal her shock. "Go to a counselor," she urged. "Don't give up, not without trying *something*."

"I'll think about it," Marlyn said halfheartedly, "but I've been so miserable lately. I'm married and I'm lonely as hell. I have a husband I see only when he can work me into his schedule."

Linc was a civil engineer. He worked for a big company that had a contract with the government for a new dam across a stream up in the mountains east of town. It was a two-hour drive over a winding road to get to town. He stayed in an RV trailer during the week and came home on weekends.

Sometimes, Krista added truthfully. Lately, he'd been tied up at work more and more on weekends. She could understand Marlyn's grief with that.

"How can he know how you feel if you don't tell him?" she asked with great practicality. "If you talk honestly with each other, that could help get your marriage back on track."

She recalled those were the words Lance Carrington had used with her. Together they were going to get the appliance company "back on track." Studying her friend, she thought things were changing in both their lives.

Change. One of the big *C*-words.

From her experience, change had often meant confusion—and chaos.

Chapter Four

Lance threw down the pen and looked at the clock. "Time to quit," he said. "I think a fourteen-hour day is long enough, don't you?"

Krista glanced at him, then back at the diagram she was working on. "Merging these two production lines will be much more efficient," she said, as if she hadn't heard him. "I want everyone cross-trained so that each person can do every job. I want them to learn to work as a team, to cover for each other if one person is out sick…or needs to take personal time—"

"Earth to Krista," he said loudly. "It's time to quit."

The conference room had spreadsheets and charts

piled on every surface. The stale odor of Chinese takeout emanated from the trash can where they'd tossed the empty cartons three hours earlier.

Friday night and they were still hard at work while the rest of the plant was silent, the employees long gone.

What, he questioned ruefully, did that say about their social lives?

Not much, was the simple answer. Krista hadn't had to call anyone to postpone a date. That was a relief in one way, but troubling in another. She was young and beautiful. She should have some fun.

He frowned when she didn't answer his summons and saw that she was still engrossed in the plans. A funny feeling rolled over him. It took him a minute to realize it was one of tenderness.

She was so earnest, so dedicated to saving the company that sometimes he wished she'd let up. He was always the one who declared it was time to go home, who summoned her from the flames of concentration that consumed her. When she left, she always took an armload of reports to read.

So did he. All that week, after she'd driven off in her jaunty red compact, he'd gone to the inn with his stack of papers to review. His room in the historic building was nice, but, well, sort of lonely.

Now when the heck had he started feeling lonely after working twelve- to fourteen-hour days?

"Let's go get a drink," he suggested, taking the production flowcharts out of her hands and placing them on the long table.

"A what?" She blinked at him as if she wasn't familiar with the term.

"A glass of warm milk to help us sleep," he said with a deadpan expression.

She laughed, then lifted her hands over her head in a spine-cracking stretch and followed that with a yawn. "I don't think I need anything. I'm dead."

"Not quite," he muttered as a different kind of hunger sneaked up on him. He couldn't help but notice the shape of her breasts as she stretched and once again had to force his mind elsewhere.

"You know something? I'm hungry. Did we eat dinner?"

"Hours ago," he reminded her. "Come on. I recently discovered the best hamburger place in town."

"Ha. I bet I know one that's better."

"We'll have to try them both, then take a vote."

They exited VIP Row, said good-night to the security guard in the lobby and went out into the cool desert night.

He inhaled deeply, glad to be out of the office. The air was sweet with sage and cactus blossoms, the sky was filled with an impossible number of stars, as if they were closer to heaven here than anywhere else on earth.

She headed toward her car at the far back of the

parking lot under the shadows of a tree. He'd had the sign with her name on the executive parking space removed one day after it was posted. She'd never used the spot.

He caught her hand to change her direction. "I'll drive," he volunteered, his voice unexpectedly husky.

She shook her head. "That's okay. I'd rather take my car. That way, I can go straight home after we eat."

"Okay, but I'll drive you out to the back forty… where you insist on parking."

After they were inside the sports car, the motor purring like a contented kitten, he paused before backing out. "If you work late, I'd be more comfortable if you had the security guard walk you to your car."

"Okay," she said absently, adjusting the seat belt to a snug fit.

"I mean it, Krista," he added in a firmer tone.

She turned her face to him, a frown gathered between her eyes. She didn't like to be ordered about, but this was important. "I said I would," she told him.

"Promise."

That focused her attention. They studied each other in the lights from the dash for a long, serious minute. When she nodded, he felt a lessening of tension.

In silence, he drove her to her car. He scanned the brush growing under the old oak and made a note to have it cleared before the weekend passed.

At the all-night diner, several cars were lined up

near the door. He chose a space where they could park side by side. She was grinning when she joined him on the sidewalk in front of the neon-lit fifties facade.

"What?" he asked warily.

"This was the place I had in mind. It does have the best hamburgers in town."

He experienced an emotion somewhere between triumph and pleasure at their mutual opinion of the food as he opened the door. "Well, great minds think alike and all that."

When she laughed, albeit wryly, he smiled, too. They chose a booth and slid into the red pseudo-leather banquettes on opposite sides of the table. He stretched his legs out. "Ahh, that feels good."

The waiter came over. "Hey, guys," he said in greeting, his gaze on Krista. "You two know what you want?"

Krista spoke up. "The number three platter, fully loaded, for me. I'll have water to drink."

"That suits me. I'll have coffee with it," Lance told the man, who slowly shambled off toward the kitchen pass-through as if he waded through molasses or something similar. "I hope he makes it before midnight."

"At least it'll be worth the wait," she said.

Lance couldn't pull his glance away when she slid her hands under her hair, then lifted her arms skyward in another luxurious stretch. Her hair fell back onto her shoulders and cupped under her chin as it tended to do.

When she closed her eyes and rested her head against the seat back, his heart went into high-speed mode, pushing hot blood to every part of his body.

She'd left her jacket in her car, so he had a clear view of the golden yellow top she wore. It fit her slender torso perfectly, outlining breasts that weren't especially large or small, but just right. Her nipples had contracted from the cooler night air and were still visible—

"Hot coffee," the waiter warned. He placed the cup on the table when Lance moved his hands aside.

Across the table, Krista opened her eyes. "I think I'd like a cup of hot chocolate," she told the man. "If you'll let me change my mind," she said in a teasing voice.

"For you, babe, anything."

It was clear that she and the man were on friendly terms. Lance discovered he didn't like that at all.

"When I worked on the production line at the plant, several of us ate here every Friday." She nodded toward the waiter as he shuffled behind the counter to prepare the cocoa. "Roger's the owner. His last name is Spaniel. I guess that's why he named the place the Doggy Diner."

Her expression was amused and so free of guile that Lance relaxed again. It was normal to feel some-what…uh…protective of her. She was his protégée, so to speak.

Since they'd had several meetings with the other executives that week, he'd observed their ambiguous manner toward her and had made it clear that he valued her ideas and opinions. When he'd backed up the production line merger over the two managers' skeptical protests, he'd noted the flash of anger in Mason's eyes.

While he didn't like the former owner's son or his attitude, Lance wasn't going to fight Krista's battles for her. If she had trouble with the man, she had to step up to the plate and do something. Like fire his butt.

When the meal arrived, Lance found himself ravenous. The hamburger was piled high with cooked onions and mushrooms, dripping with cheese and a special sauce on a crusty bun. The baked potato was equally decadent with sour cream, chives and bacon bits. A huge onion ring crowned the whole thing while a slice of tomato and a leaf of lettuce were tucked to one side. He added those to the hamburger.

"Open wide," she advised when he lifted the overstuffed concoction.

He had to smile as she tried to do the same. She had to lick the sauce and cheese off her lips before she could proceed. After several attempts, she gave up and swiped across her mouth with the napkin.

"Heavenly," she murmured after swallowing.

He tried not to stare while they ate, but it was damn difficult. He wanted to taste those lips, to share her enjoyment on a more intimate level....

Lance finished eating first. Roger poured him a fresh cup of coffee and he concentrated on that while Krista ate every bite of the dinner.

"Oh, I'm stuffed," she groaned, pushing her plate aside. "Roger, that was delicious as usual."

"Thank you, ma'am. You want another cup of chocolate?"

She shook her head and gave the man a dazzling smile. The weariness had disappeared, Lance saw, and her cheeks once more held a healthy glow. When she yawned, he stood up and tossed some bills on the table. "Let's go before you fall asleep, and I have to cart you out."

She lifted one eyebrow at the rueful note. Little does she know, he thought, sensing his own weariness and knowing it would disappear in a flash if she but gave him the word.

"Thanks for the treat," she said, smiling up at him after she was inside her vehicle.

"Yeah, no problem." He pointed at the car. "Lock the doors."

The tiny dimples, which he realized could express joy or exasperation with equal aplomb, appeared, but she did as he ordered. "Eight in the morning?" she asked.

He nodded. "We'll finish that flow chart, then I'm heading back to Denver. You can start merging the lines and see how it goes."

She laughed softly. "Problems you never thought of have a way of cropping up. But I'm sure we'll manage."

"One of my top advisors will be available if you need him. He's a financial whiz, too. You two will get along like a house afire," he added, a sudden vision of Toby's blond hair close to her dark tresses as they worked out accounting and manufacturing processes.

"I look forward to meeting him," she said politely, her eyes holding a trace of doubt.

Watching her drive off, Lance followed at a safe distance, then turned right toward the inn when she went left and crossed the bridge over the river.

He tried to suppress the desire to cart her off into the night. Right to his comfy bed at the inn.

That, as all the business tomes advised, was not a good idea. Maybe if they'd met under different circumstances, nature could take its course.

She was certainly attractive, and they had a lot in common. They both liked flashy red cars and juicy hamburgers. They were both good at their jobs.

They'd been hurt by life. She'd spent a year in the mountains hiding out from the welfare people. He and his parents had spent nearly two years on the run, hiding out from his grandfather.

For a moment, he let himself remember—his parents' happiness when they were on the upside of alcohol, the remorse when they hit the downside and there was no money to buy more. His mother's promise that day in the corridor of the courthouse.

We'll get you back. We'll change. You'll see.

He'd left the street for a life of luxury…and loneliness. He'd waited, but his parents hadn't changed, hadn't come for him. Instead, they'd died within six months of each other, the promise forgotten….

Something within himself had also died during that long cold winter of his tenth year. He'd thought if he wished hard enough, if he was really good and really tried hard enough, then all would be well. His parents would get better, they would come for him and he'd have a happy home like the families on TV sitcoms.

Both he and Krista had learned that life didn't follow a script. He gave a snort of bitter laughter. Eventually he'd realized that he could depend on no one but himself. His world would be what *he* made of it.

Krista had returned from the wilderness to a place that had provided love and security. Lucky her.

Krista returned to her apartment complex shortly before lunch on Saturday. Lance was leaving for Denver that afternoon, and he'd insisted she take the rest of the weekend off. Smiling, she parked under the carport in her assigned space and walked along the pleasant, winding path to her town house. The maid service had been in the previous day, so after making a grocery list and doing the shopping, she was at loose ends.

Taking a book and an insulated mug of iced tea, she went to the swimming pool and did some laps, then tried to read. But the story didn't hold her attention. Life, she thought, was much more interesting.

Monday was to be the big day.

She and Lance and the two production managers had discussed the coming changes that morning. She'd explained how the regular toaster and oven toaster lines were to be merged while the production process continued.

She was a little nervous since it was her idea. Other changes were in the works.

Lance hadn't said a word about personnel, but she knew the plant had to become more efficient. She was also sure that during the six-month period she'd agreed to stay, she was under the microscope in regard to her managing skills.

He was good about backing her up, but her career depended on her making correct decisions. That included getting rid of excess workers, which added up to around three hundred people.

Thank goodness she had a plan, one that would be as fair to everyone as possible. She was going to ask for a very good retirement package for those employees sixty and over. Coupled with the natural attrition of those leaving to take other jobs and so forth, that should do the trick.

Satisfied that this was the best solution, she called her uncle and aunt and told them how the first week had gone with the new boss.

"I feel as if I've been through a whole semester of an advanced business course," she told them. "If there are any holes in my ideas or reports, the new CEO sees them at once, then he asks questions that actually point out the weak places. He's just like Uncle Jeff," she told Caileen, who was on the kitchen phone while her uncle was out in his shop on the portable.

The women laughed while he defended his fellow men. "Can we help it if we're inclined by nature to be completely logical?" he demanded in a lofty tone.

"Ask him how logical he was when some nut nearly ran us off the road the other day," Caileen suggested.

"Are you okay?" Krista asked.

"We're fine thanks to your uncle's quick reflexes behind the wheel."

"Oh, good. Well, I think I'll take a nap since we've been working until nine or ten every night this week."

After they hung up, she pulled her knees up, wrapped her arms around them and gazed absently at the landscape while she thought about her life of late.

She was having fun. Really.

There was something about being in the thick of things, making decisions, being taken seriously, putting ideas into action…. These all made work much more exciting.

And Lance Carrington? Did he make work more exciting?

Yes. He was a good boss. He listened. He asked questions that made her think instead of treating her like an inexperienced twit. In the areas where she wasn't sure what to do, he provided guidance without giving orders.

Except when it came to walking across the dark parking lot and locking her car doors.

He was unexpectedly protective then. When he'd made her promise to have the guard walk her to her car, it had given her a feeling of being…cared for or something.

Nah. He probably didn't want a lawsuit over employee security if something terrible happened to her.

Shaking her head at her wandering thoughts, she went inside, showered and changed into pajamas. She was in for the night. A stack of reports awaited her review.

On Wednesday, Krista searched through the conference room for the notes she'd made on the production line merger. There was one thing she wanted to change, and she was sure she'd made a note of it. If she hadn't, Lance probably had.

Going into his office, she stood behind the desk and glanced over its pristine surface. Hmm, when had he put things away?

While he didn't keep a cluttered desk, he did like items he was working on placed in neat stacks close at hand.

The same as she did.

After checking the in- and out-baskets, she opened the desk drawers and quickly glanced through them. She had no qualms about doing this, as Lance had given her a key to the desk and she'd gotten reports from it several times during the past week. Actually he'd told her to move in to the larger, more impressive space, but she hadn't quite been able to bring herself to do that.

For one thing, there was the problem of secretaries. If Tiff was her secretary, what did she do with Thea?

Krista gave a soft snort. If only James had taken the old dragon with him—

"What are you doing?" a sharp voice snapped, nearly causing her to drop the files she had in hand.

"Hello, Thea," she replied, refusing to sound guilty. "I'm looking for some notes Lance and I made the other day."

"What are those files?" Thea questioned. "What are you doing with them?"

Krista waved the files rather airily. "I'm going to study these before the staff meeting next Monday."

Thea came around the desk. "Let me see." She held out her hand in an imperious manner. "Some files aren't allowed to leave the office."

Krista riffled through the personnel folders as if she didn't see the hand. "Actually," she said firmly, "these are my files now." She glanced up with a smile. "Lance says this is my office, too, but I haven't had time to move. Ah, there's the legal pad."

She reached past the secretary, who stood as if turned to stone, and grabbed the pad off the credenza. Lance's neat notations beside her own handwriting had an immediate calming effect on her.

Gathering the material into an orderly stack, she looked at Thea with a questioning smile. "Was there something you needed?" she asked politely.

A red flush climbed the other woman's neck. She walked out of the office and closed the door firmly behind her.

Krista sank back into the big executive chair and let out a long, slow breath. The top personnel folder was labeled with the secretary's name. Krista was going to review it and all the managers' files who'd been there a long time with an eye toward retirement. Before she approached Lance with the buyout package, she planned to have all her ducks in a row.

One thing that would help with the finances: Mason was going to be cut to an appropriate salary for the work he did.

The phone rang. She saw it was the private line into the office. She answered.

"Hi," Lance's deep voice said. "Your secretary said you were looting the office."

Krista laughed. "I'm stealing some of the personnel files. Thea caught me. I thought she was going to make me stand in the corner for snooping."

There was a slight pause. "Have you thought about what you're going to do about her and others who may not be needed after the changes are made?"

She took a deep breath. "Yes. Do you have time to listen?"

"Shoot," he invited.

Crossing one leg over her knee and resting against the soft, worn leather, she realized, as she explained her plan to decrease the employees without laying anyone off, that she missed having him close, having the doors to the conference room open between their offices as they worked.

"That's good," he said at one point. "I don't think we'll have any trouble convincing my board to accept the retirement plan."

"Uh, your board?" she said.

"That's why I called. They want to meet you. There's a museum benefit auction Friday night. I thought we would have dinner with a couple of CCS board members, then go to the benefit. You'll get a chance to meet Toby before he comes down to Grand Junction next week. If you're free for the weekend," he added.

"I don't know. Let me check with my computer and see if it can give me the night off," she quipped.

His chuckle sent a tingle up and down her spine, a feeling she did her best to ignore.

"It's a three-hour trip by car," he told her. "There's a flight you can get at four on Friday afternoon. I'll pick you up at the airport here. Also, there's a nice inn near the office that serves a hot breakfast. I'll have my secretary book you a room."

"Thanks," she said.

He must have heard the hesitancy in her voice. "What?" he asked.

"When am I coming back here?"

"Good question. I've scheduled a full board meeting with you on Monday morning. Let's see, you'll be here, mmm, three nights—Friday, Saturday and Sunday. You can check out of the inn on Monday morning when I pick you up."

"I'll cancel the staff meeting here," she told him. "We're in the middle of merging the production lines."

"How's that going?"

"No problems, actually. We had a conference with the employees and explained things. Most of them liked the idea of cross-training and working as a team. Only a few were unsure about it."

He understood at once. "Change is harder on the older workers."

And sometimes on the younger ones, she thought, reminded of her own chaotic life.

"What time should I get a flight out on Monday?" she asked.

"I'm coming back down there after the board meeting here, so you may as well ride back with me. It'll probably be pretty late Monday before we get back to Grand Junction," he warned.

"Okay. I've marked my calendar," she said.

After they hung up, she stayed in the big chair and gazed at the loveliness of the spring day through the wall of windows. The comfortable chair seemed to embrace her like a pair of loving arms.

Ha. She was twenty-five and she hadn't had a date in a year. In fact she hadn't had a real relationship since breaking up with her boyfriend in college.

The pain of that moment came back to her. He'd accused her of trying to hold on when it was obvious to both of them it was time to let go. He'd said she smothered him with her clinging ways.

At the time she'd felt as if she'd fallen into a vat of humiliation. Keeping a firm grip on her pride, she'd helped him find any lost items he'd left at her place and wished him well as he walked out the door.

Thanks to Caileen, she understood separation anxiety. From a childhood in which it seemed people were always abandoning her and her brother, it was natural to want to hold on to the status quo. Children needed stability.

However, as Caileen had explained, discussing a relationship wasn't clinging to a hopeless situation. It was the adult way of dealing with the differences that existed between people, no matter how much they loved each other.

So good riddance, she mentally told her former steady. It took two to make things work.

He'd certainly been glad to accept her help on his essays and term papers, which she'd edited for errors. She'd drawn the line at writing them for him, which hadn't pleased him at all. His concept of their relationship seemed to be that she should put in the most effort.

That was why working with Lance was such a revelation. They really did work together as a team.

Yawning, she snuggled deeper into the chair and rested the folders in her lap. Turning her face into the leather, she caught the slightest whiff of Lance's aftershave. A current ran through her as if someone had flipped a switch.

It reminded her of joy, and excitement.

Funny, she hadn't felt like that in a long time.

Chapter Five

"Are you nervous?" Marlyn asked.

Krista shrugged. "A little. Meeting the CCS board is one of those necessary evils. I knew it was coming."

She and her friend were having a late lunch on Friday, then Marlyn was driving her to the community airport for the flight to Denver.

"How are things going with the raider?" Marlyn asked.

Krista laughed. "Great. If that's the word to describe fourteen-hour days hunched over flowcharts and spreadsheets." She explained about actually getting to put one of her ideas into practice. "Combining the two production lines is working like a charm." She ate a bite of chicken pot pie. "How are things going with you and Linc?"

"Not great."

Krista felt a helpless anger with Marlyn's thoughtless husband. Linc wasn't deliberately mean, but he certainly didn't catch on to the responsibilities of having a life partner, in her opinion. "Did you talk to him?"

"Yeah."

"What did he say?"

"He doesn't have time for *all that*. He thinks I should understand that he has a tough job and he has to be there. He thinks I should have moved up there with him."

Krista was shocked. "How Neanderthal," she murmured. "You can't run your business from the mountains."

"That's just it. He thinks I should have closed the shop."

Although Marlyn waved her fork airily, Krista saw her anger and frustration in the set of her mouth and the way the insouciance didn't quite reach her eyes.

"I know," Krista said, getting an idea, "you need to give Linc a clue on how couples cooperate."

"How's that?" Marlyn asked, more than a tad cynical.

"What if you go up after closing the shop and stay

with him for the weekend? Maybe he'll get the hint to do the same next weekend."

"Huh. I'd have to hit him with a baseball bat to get that idea across."

"Think about it," Krista urged. "Tell him you want to take turns visiting on weekends. It'll be fun, like having a honeymoon every week."

Marlyn rolled her eyes, then gave Krista a keen study. "Girlfriend, are you falling in love with the raider?"

Krista thought of all the hours she and Lance had spent together the previous week, practically living at the office. The sense of being in tune, of working toward a common goal, bred a closeness that was deceptive. It wasn't something she was used to, so it would be easy to think there was more between them than business. That would be foolish.

"You think I'm stupid?" Krista demanded.

"Okay, just asking, but you sure are seeing things through the rose-hued glasses these days."

Krista grimaced. "Separation anxiety. I always want things to work out and everyone to be happy."

Marlyn's flippant pose wilted. "Dream on," she said, deep unhappiness evident in her face. "Don't fall in love. It isn't good for the heart." She checked the time. "We'd better hurry. You need to be at the airport an hour early to get through security."

* * *

On the short flight to Denver, Krista tried to figure out why two people who supposedly loved each other couldn't have separate goals as well as common ones and help each other achieve them. She'd read the books her aunt had recommended on relationships, but no one seemed to follow their suggestions. Maybe modern life was just too hard.

Recalling her own past, she knew her mom had loved her stepfather and he'd loved her, but he'd followed the rodeo and ranching circuits. After almost ten years, her mom had said she couldn't travel around the country like gypsies any longer, so they'd divorced. The stable life her mother had envisioned had ended in tragedy within a year.

Lesson: Life is unpredictable.

Did that mean a person should grab at happiness when it came along? Or was it wiser—and safer— to guard the heart from potential pain?

She was still mulling over this conundrum when the plane landed. Walking through the security area, she spotted Lance waiting on the other side.

Her heart kicked around in her chest like the bucking broncos her stepdad used to ride.

"Good flight?" he asked, taking her bag and pulling it along behind them.

"Yes, fine."

He had a town car with a driver waiting at the curb. "I didn't know how much luggage you would have."

The driver stored her one bag in the roomy trunk.

"For a weekend?" she said.

Lance and the driver chuckled. "Yeah. Sorry. I had a stereotypical view of women travelers."

"Apology accepted."

Although she smiled, her thoughts remained in a quagmire of worry about male-female relationships. Lance was her boss, so she'd better watch herself. She wouldn't be stupid and fall in love.

There. That was a simple plan, an easy one to follow.

Lance glanced at his watch, then at the stairs. He'd arrived at the inn a couple of minutes ago after calling Krista on the cell phone to tell her he was on his way. If they didn't get moving, they'd be late.

At that moment, a woman appeared at the head of the elegant staircase. He sucked in a harsh breath as Krista descended with a calm smile on her face.

She wore a long black skirt that flowed gently around her ankles and hinted at long, shapely legs clad in black stockings, which he could glimpse each time she moved down one more step in her black heels.

A black jacket covered a form-fitting black top shot with gold threads. Her hair was held up on the back of her head with two Chinese combs in red, black and gold. Long, dangly earrings sparkled on her ears, touching a spot on her neck that he wanted to kiss, to nibble on….

His body was filled with a shock of undiluted lust. He forced himself to move two steps forward and hold out his arm to her. "Good evening. You look gorgeous."

Her smile was muted, no sign of the dimples. "Thank you. I wasn't sure how businesslike I was supposed to look for this event."

"You're perfect," he said, his tone unintentionally brusque.

He took her arm and escorted her to the sports car parked under the inn's portico. After they were on their way to the dinner scheduled with two senior members of the board of directors and their wives, he managed to make small talk.

"A cold front is supposed to move through the area. I put a fleece throw behind your seat in case you need it."

He groaned as he rattled on like a teenager on a date with the most popular girl in school and changed the subject to the board members she would soon meet.

They arrived at the restaurant just as the other guests did and were shown to a reserved table where Lance made the introductions.

"How do you do?" Krista said politely, her manner poised, as if she hobnobbed with two of the richest families in the country all the time. He had to smile as pride had him acting like a hen with a prize chick.

"So how's the line merger going?" one of the men asked when they were seated and had ordered cocktails.

Krista's stunning smile nearly stopped Lance's heart.

"Great." She told of the meeting with the employees to explain what was taking place.

Lance relaxed as Krista and the others engaged in a lively discussion which ranged over several topics in the course of the meal. Mission accomplished. He'd wanted her to be familiar with two of the most influential members of the board before walking into a full meeting cold on Monday morning. Later tonight, she'd meet Toby, who could charm the whiskers off a cat.

Hmm, maybe he'd better keep an eye on his best friend, make sure he didn't sweep her off her feet.

Shortly after nine, they arrived at the museum. The first person he noticed when they went inside was Jenna. Thinking he would be out of town, he'd canceled his obligation to escort her to the event. She didn't look very happy to see him. Damn, he'd forgotten to call her and let her know he was attending after all.

"Lance, glad you could make it," Toby called out. He handed Jenna a glass of champagne and guided her over. "Ah, this must be Krista," he said, taking Krista's hand and bowing gallantly over it.

"This is Toby Branigan, the financial wizard I told you about," Lance told Krista. "And this is a longtime friend, Jenna Walters. You met John and Mary Walters at dinner. They're Jenna's grandparents. Krista had to come up for a board meeting," he explained to Jenna to erase the darts shooting from her blue eyes, "so I thought she should come early so she and Toby could go over some reports."

"Oh, you're the wunderkind from Grand Junction," Jenna said, her mouth relaxing into a true smile.

"Well, I am from there, but I don't know about the other," Krista said modestly. She glanced around. "I've been to the museum here once before and loved it. Is the new wing open? I like sculpture. My uncle works in metal, mostly copper. Naturally I love his pieces."

Jenna nodded. "My mother and I are cosponsors of tonight's events. Which means we coerce money out of our friends." She laughed and gave Lance a flirtatious glance from under her lashes. "Lance has given me permission to buy something from the auction in his name."

"How nice," Krista said, giving him an approving look.

"What is your uncle's name?" Jenna asked. "Perhaps we have something from him."

Lance kept a smile on his face, but inside he seethed. Jenna's superior attitude grated on him. Her manner clearly indicated she didn't expect to recognize Krista's uncle.

"Jefferson Aquilon," Krista answered without the slightest change in her calm, smiling manner.

"Jefferson..." Jenna spluttered to a halt. "As it happens, we do have a piece by him, donated by one of the museum directors."

Krista's eyes gleamed. "Oh, could we see it, do you think?"

Lance noted that Jenna's smile became rather grim around the edges as the evening wore on. Krista, on the other hand, seemed totally at ease as she discussed her uncle's sculpture and skills with the director, who was delighted to meet her.

"Do you think he will continue his work in copper?" the man's wife asked. "His feminine pieces in copper are absolutely splendid."

"Copper is his favorite medium," Krista replied, "but he also works in mixed metals. Have you seen his caricatures? They're hilarious...and becoming quite the collector's item. Everyone back home wants to pose for one."

"Your protégée is something," Toby said in an aside to Lance while the others walked to the next exhibit. "The fair Jenna is turning green."

"Thanks for your help in keeping things light," Lance said. "I should have warned Jenna I would be coming and bringing someone. My mistake. I don't want Krista hurt because of it."

"You underestimate her. She handles herself very well," Toby told him with a sly smile.

Lance nodded. "It's late. When does the auction start?"

"Now," Jenna said, stepping close and catching the last part of the conversation.

Another ninety minutes passed before Lance could escort Krista from the gala. To his surprise, she bought a small piece, a sculpture made of ipe wood that looked like ribbons coming from the base and joined at the top.

"It reminds me of the Maypole dances they made us do at school. It was the passion of the English teacher that we get it right. Every year the students got hopelessly tangled. It became a rite of passage for the sixth graders."

He chuckled as he started the engine. The clock on the dash indicated it was just past midnight.

He glanced at Krista as he headed for the inn and saw her chest lift in a long drawn breath. She exhaled the same way, as if she was utterly weary.

"It's been a long day for you," he said, a sort of apology for keeping her up so late, and for subjecting her to Jenna's slight barbs.

Those he hadn't expected. While he and the socialite had dated some over the past six months, he'd never considered it an exclusive relationship. Neither had he accepted the invitation in her eyes to carry it further.

Truthfully, she didn't attract him enough to put up with her demanding ways.

He glanced at his companion. She was the exception to almost every rule he'd ever made about combining business and pleasure. He was attracted to her on every level.

Including the emotional one.

That was the tricky part. After his parents' deaths, his grandmother had filled the empty places in his life until she, too, died, of breast cancer when he was twenty-one. She'd been the reason he hadn't left his grandfather's house long before that.

Since then he'd had two long-term relationships, but those had ended when he'd rejected the idea of marriage and family. He didn't want responsibility for another's happiness. Most of all, he didn't want to bring children into the world. He'd seen what could happen to those who were too young or helpless or poor to fight back. He'd been all three at various times in his life.

The chill of the night seemed to penetrate right to his bones. He forced the past back into its cold locker as he pulled into the shadows under the inn's portico.

Soft lights around the driveway and in the lobby welcomed latecomers, although no one appeared to be up.

"Am I your protégée?" Krista asked, her tone guarded.

"Where did you get that idea?"

"Toby. That's what he called me when you and Jenna were discussing an auction piece she wanted to bid on."

Lance got the vibes from her. She didn't like the idea. At the moment, he wasn't in the mood for sparring with her. He wanted warmth, the lithe strength of her body, the sweetness of her touch...

"A mentor is considered a good thing, according to the business gurus," he told her.

She sat in stiff silence for a few seconds. "Yes, I suppose it is."

"But you resent it." He unsnapped the seat belt and leaned close to her, his defense against temptation and stupidity eroding rapidly.

She turned her face to his and met his gaze. "It makes the other person subordinate to the mentor."

"You want equality," he murmured, seeing in her the stubborn independence his grandfather had often derided in him.

"I want to be treated as a business associate with a mind of my own. I know I don't have a lot of experience, but I have ideas and...and plans."

The hesitation at the end of her little speech brought on the tenderness. He cupped his hand under her chin, feeling the smoothness of her skin against his palm.

"You have good ideas. You're great at making

plans," he agreed, unable to keep the huskiness out of his voice.

Then he did a foolish thing.

He kissed her.

Her lips were as soft as they looked, and so enticing. When they opened in a startled gasp, he warned himself not to take advantage, not to take it further.

But temptation was too great.

He had to experience the sweetness of her mouth for himself. One taste, then he would draw back, wish her a casual goodnight, as if this was the natural conclusion of the evening.

That's what he meant to do. That's what he *ordered* himself to do. It wasn't what he did.

With a groan, he pressed closer, intending to wrap her in his embrace and take all she would give—

Before he could act on the impulse, she raised her hands and pushed against his chest. At the same time, she turned her head so the kiss was broken.

For a second he experienced a sharp sense of emptiness, one he hadn't felt in years. Not since the day his grandfather led him out of a big brick courthouse and his life had changed forever.

"Don't," she said, her expression uncertain for a split second before changing to a definite glare.

He sucked in a ragged breath. "Sorry. It just seemed like the right way to end the evening."

That much was true. He didn't think it wise to

add it was also the result of an overpowering impulse. Another truth, but one he didn't think she would believe.

Krista read the Denver news while eating her usual cereal with nonfat milk on Saturday morning. The inn baked its own bread and pastries, and the aroma filling the place was heavenly. She'd resisted all but the apple dumpling, which was wrapped in its own flaky crust and floated in a cinnamon-caramel sauce.

"What decadence," a deep masculine voice said, "dessert with breakfast."

She looked into gray eyes that gave her a quick assessment as Lance smiled at her. She returned the smile, but it was difficult.

Last night, instead of accepting the brief kiss as a casual good-night—which was his intention, she was sure—she'd scrambled out of the car like a startled doe and run for her life, her lips on fire and her thoughts scattered in all directions.

"I'll have the apple pastry," he now said to the waitress, "and coffee."

"That's your breakfast?" Krista asked in the same tone he'd used.

"I ate hours ago."

"Oh." She glanced at the clock behind the inn's reception desk. Almost ten. She'd slept late, unable to settle down once she'd gone to bed last night, actually around one this morning, she corrected.

"Did you sleep well?" he asked, taking a chair beside her. Again he surveyed her face as if looking for cracks in her composure.

"Yes. Eventually," she added in total honesty.

"I didn't mean to upset you last night."

His voice was soft, quiet with portent, like the moments before dawn broke and a new day arrived. She felt his concern for her, the naïf who didn't know how to accept a simple kiss without panicking.

"You didn't, that is, I wasn't prepared...I just didn't expect—" She stopped before she made a complete fool of herself.

"Let's chalk it up to the late hour, a pleasant evening and the fact that you looked irresistible."

Her nerves lurched at the backhanded compliment. She frowned at him. "Fine, but let's keep the line between mentor and protégée clearly in place."

"By all means."

She studied him as he gazed out the window. There was a tension about him, a grimness that didn't quite disappear when he smiled. He obviously regretted the impromptu kiss.

That answered the question about his reaction and the deep, hidden meaning behind the embrace that had plagued her during the wee hours of the morning. There hadn't been one.

The kiss had obviously been a friendly farewell gesture for him. The shock of it—the soft pressure of his mouth on hers, the warmth of his lips, the gentleness as he glided over her lips to find the perfect fit—had made it seem more to her.

It had been blessedly brief, or else she might have melted in his arms. Or worse, kissed him back.

That was part of the problem that had kept her awake long after she went to bed—the fact that she'd wanted to sink into his embrace and return his kiss...and a thousand more.

She obliquely observed him while he chatted with the waitress about the cold front that was moving through, then looked away as he focused his attention back on her.

"Mmm, delicious," he said, taking a bite of the apple dumpling. "Are you finished with the front page?"

Nodding, she kept eating until she'd finished every bite of the meal. That way she didn't have to talk. Over coffee, they both caught up on the news. He commented about the article he was reading a couple of times.

The scene reminded her of weekend breakfasts with Jeff and Caileen. They, too, had read the paper and chatted about the news. Jeremy and Zia were at college by then, but she and Tony had read the comics, feeling very adult as they lingered at the table with the other two.

It had been a peaceful time in their lives. Serene. And safe. Safe, a simple four-letter word, but it had formed the basis of her life with her foster uncle and aunt.

Oddly, that was the way she felt now with Lance, in spite of the turmoil caused by the kiss. Gazing into the steam rising from her coffee cup, she wondered if he had ever felt insecure, had ever not known where his next meal was coming from—

"Are you planning a big business coup?"

She jerked at the interruption, sloshing a couple of drops of coffee on the white tablecloth.

"You looked so serious, I thought you were planning on taking over CCS and ousting me," he continued wryly.

That made her smile. "Not until I've learned everything you know," she assured him.

His laughter had its usual effect on her. How could something be soothing and exciting at the same time?

"So what are we doing today, boss?" she asked, regaining a firm footing with the title.

"Going to the office. Are you ready?"

She nodded.

Twenty minutes later, they walked into an impressive downtown office building. CCS commanded the top floor.

Lance's office, on the northwest corner, looked out on a panorama of the front range of the Rocky Mountains. Below them, she had a view of a street that had been made into a pedestrian walk with trees and places to sit and lots of restaurants.

"My gosh, I'd never get any work done," she told him. "I'd be gazing out the windows all the time."

He came over. "I like looking at the mountains," he admitted. "Sometimes it's snowing on the peaks, so it's like gazing into a snow globe after you give it a good shake."

Her attention was no longer on the vista, but on the contact between her shoulder and his chest as he pointed out rocky crags and named the passes between them.

The hunger from last night rose like a well filled to overflowing by spring rains. Emotions, too quick to name, flooded her with yearning as well as sexual heat, which she recognized for what it was, she admitted ruefully.

Since becoming CFO of the appliance company, she'd concentrated all her energy on financial and marketing strategies to stave off bankruptcy, but business was far from her mind at present.

She wanted fulfillment.

Her breasts ached as the longing grew. She wanted him to take her into his arms...

"Yo," a voice called out from the outer office.

Lance moved away. "That's Toby," he told her. "Come on in," he called out.

Krista was so relieved to see another person she

could have hugged him. The irony of that thought brought a true smile to her face as she greeted the financial expert.

"I've gone over your production line ideas," he told her, settling into business as soon as the greetings were over and all had agreed the museum benefit had been fun.

Except for Jenna. Krista hadn't been able to decipher the relationship between the other woman and Lance. That was probably why the unexpected good-night kiss had alarmed her so. She didn't want to cause problems for anyone—

"Let's go into the conference room," Lance suggested.

Krista was at ease right away. This was her domain. She understood spreadsheets and charts. Reports didn't demand an analysis, or a rationalization, of odd emotions that impeded the thinking processes.

For the next three hours, she and Toby went over every appliance Heymyer produced—toasters, toaster ovens, microwave ovens, mixers, blenders, coffeemakers.

"I want a new coffeemaker," she told the men. "I want to be able to hook it up to a water supply, toss a pound of coffee into the machine and have it measure out the correct amount of each, then perk at a preset time."

"Are you suggesting we put computers in coffeemakers?" Lance asked, clutching his chest as if in shock.

Toby glanced from one to the other. "So?" he asked.

Krista burst out laughing. Lance joined in. The more they laughed, the funnier it seemed.

"I must have missed the stand-up comedy routine," Toby muttered.

That set the other two off again.

"Just one of my dingbat notions," Krista finally explained.

"Yes, we've got to watch her on those," Lance chimed in. "We draw the line at computers in appliances."

Toby shook his head as they laughed again. Krista knew he was wondering what was going on between them, especially when he gave Lance a hard stare, then raised his eyebrows at his friend.

The boss merely grinned, then ignored the question in the gesture. Well, Krista thought, there was nothing to tell. Truly.

They had lunch in the middle of the afternoon. Lance left them after asking Toby to drive her back to the inn.

"So, where did you go to school?" Toby asked. "Start at the beginning and tell me your life story."

She finished off the last quarter of the club sandwich and settled back in the comfortable chair. "I was on a work/study program for the undergraduate degree, then did the MBA through the university program here in Colorado. You don't sound as if you're from around here," she added.

"Boston, originally. Lance and I were at Princeton at the same time. He told me if I signed on to his business venture, he would make me rich."

"Sounds like a deal."

"I told him I was already rich—inheritance and all that, you know," he said with pseudo-modesty.

"Oh, sure."

They grinned at each other.

"But you decided to throw your fate and fortune in with him anyway?" she asked.

"Yeah. He does the big picture. I like the nitty-gritty stuff."

"Uh, yes, he explained the division of labor in much the same way to me back in Grand Junction."

Toby studied her for a long twenty seconds before smiling in a way that made her suspicious of what he was thinking. "You're going to be good for him."

Not sure how to respond to that, she changed the subject to the weather.

But later, back at the inn, she recalled Toby's words about her being good for Lance. She wondered if the corporate raider was going to be good for her.

Career-wise? Possibly.

Heart-wise? Don't even think about it.

Chapter Six

"Do you always take your out-of-town executives on a sightseeing tour?" Krista asked, settling into a four-wheel drive SUV shortly before noon on Sunday.

"Actually, I do," Lance assured her. "It doesn't seem very cordial to invite someone in for a staff meeting, then leave them to their own devices during the off-hours."

"That's thoughtful," she murmured, not sure whether she felt insulted or relieved that she wasn't getting special treatment.

Although she kept her eyes on the scenery as they went ever higher into the mountains, she was very aware of his masculine presence. It was, she found, becoming difficult to keep her business life separate from the personal.

That kiss, she mused in despair. It was going to cause trouble. Maybe not for him, but definitely for her.

The problem was that she took life too seriously. She didn't know how to be casual about a relationship. Could she indulge her sensual side without engaging the emotional? Or would she once again smother a man with her clinging ways?

The hurt of that accusation returned, bringing with it a renewed sense of caution and a vow to maintain the proper attitude toward her mentor, boss, whatever he was.

She sensed a barrier around the corporate raider that kept a distance between him and any deep relationship. Like her, he'd learned to be cautious. He would never allow anyone to cling for long.

She inhaled deeply, drawing into her lungs the scent of the forest and the sea that seemed to come from him. Every nerve ending in her body tingled with passionate hunger and the need to be in his arms, to feel his lips in a real kiss, one that went beyond a casual good-night.

Dear heavens, how was she going to make it for six months when she was already on the edge of an abyss?

"Are you worried about the meeting with the board tomorrow?" he asked.

"Not really. It's a bit intimidating, but so were the orals for the MBA. One survives." She managed a brief laugh.

"Most people do," he said grimly. "Some don't."

Not sure what they were talking about, she made a noncommittal sound and remained quiet.

"There's a pub about five miles up the road. We'll have lunch there. It has a really great view of the mountains."

"That sounds nice." She silently groaned at how stilted she sounded.

Before he could reply, his cell phone rang. He checked the calling number, frowned, then hit the talk button.

The other person did most of the talking, but listening to Lance's terse questions, she understood that something serious had happened.

"We're going to have to head back to the city," he said upon ending the call. "My grandfather has had an episode with his heart. He refuses to go to the hospital. The doctor doesn't think it's life-threatening, but the old man needs to be checked out."

"I'm so sorry. I hope he'll be okay."

Lance turned around at the next pull-out. "His home is on this side of town. Do you mind if we stop?"

"No, not at all. I can get a taxi back to the inn."

"Let's see what's happening first."

The trip down the mountain took forty minutes.

On the outskirts of town, he turned onto a paved county road, then right onto a winding drive a couple of miles after that.

"Oh," she said when the house suddenly came into view.

"Impressive, huh?"

There was an undercurrent of grimness, almost contempt, in the question that she didn't understand. She knew he'd lived with his grandparents from the time he was ten and his parents had died within a few months of each other. The interview she'd read hadn't revealed more than that.

Like her, he'd lost those he loved the most at an early age. She felt the bond of those losses stretch between them, the cords of grief and fear that children, helpless against a world turned upside down, experienced. Death touched all families, even the very rich.

She surveyed the brick and stone mansion as he drove around the circular driveway, then parked at the side. Wide steps led up to French doors.

"Shall I wait here?" she asked.

"No. I don't know how long we'll be." He smiled at her. "You won't be in the way."

Nodding, she climbed out when he did and went up the steps. A man was already at the set of double doors. "Mr. Lance," he said. "It's good to see you."

"Morgan," Lance said in greeting when they entered and the doors were closed against the cold air. The two shook hands. "Morgan and his wife take care of the house and everyone in it. Ms. Aquilon is a business associate."

Krista spoke to the older man, who was dressed in black slacks and a white shirt with a black tie. He appeared to be in his late fifties.

"The doctor called you?" Morgan asked, his expression anxious. "I asked him to. I think things are more serious than Mr. Claude lets on."

"Yes, he called. He wants to admit Grandfather to the clinic and do a thorough check. I told him I'd speak to the old mule about it."

Krista noted the servant didn't bat an eye at the reference to his employer.

"Ah, good."

"My grandfather is as stubborn as others I could name," Lance said on a lighter note with a smile in her direction. "Where is he?" he asked the other man.

"In the library. He insisted on coming down. I built a fire, and he's in the recliner. He was asleep when I checked on him a few minutes ago."

"Thanks. I'll look in on him." He gestured toward her. "Would you show Krista to the sitting room? She might like a cup of tea. Or hot chocolate."

"I'm fine. I don't need anything."

Lance nodded and crossed the entrance hall, which had marble tiles and was as large as her living room.

"This way, miss," Morgan said.

She went with him down a long hallway of richly paneled wood, with statues and vases in niches. Dignified portraits—Lance's ancestors?—graced the walls.

When Morgan indicated she was to precede him into a room at the end of the hall, she quickly did so. "How lovely," she said in surprise.

The sitting room had windows on two sides and was decorated in soft shades of pink and beige with splashes of green. The colors were repeated in the carpet. A green chenille sofa invited one to lounge, maybe indulge in an afternoon nap. A matching love seat and two floral chairs completed the conversation area.

"Would you like a fire?" the servant asked.

She didn't want to put the man to any extra work on her account. "No, thank you. It's quite comfortable in here."

"There are books and magazines on the shelves and in the baskets." He pointed to the bookshelves on either side of the fireplace and two baskets filled with periodicals beside the chairs.

"Thank you. I'll be fine."

After he left, she walked around the cozy room, which seemed at odds with the formality of the entrance and hallway.

The windows framed views that were just beginning to show signs of spring. The bright green of tender grass was visible in the lawn. Flower beds bloomed with the purple and gold of crocus blossoms while stalks of daffodils waved in the chilly breeze off the mountain, their blossoms swelling but not yet open. By May, the grounds would be dazzling.

Choosing a magazine on horticulture, she sat on the sofa and tried to imagine a ten-year-old boy running down that long, austere hallway.

Had he been reprimanded? Or sent outside to play, as her mom had done with her and her brother? Often, her stepdad had gone outside, too, and joined them, usually for a game of Frisbee.

"You're good," her stepfather would say when she or Tony made a especially good catch. He'd wink at her mom, who often came out and sat on the steps to watch.

She suddenly missed them, her mother, brother and stepfather, with an aching misery that delved deep into her soul. Jeremy and his dad had often visited, too. She'd loved every one of them with all her nine-year-old heart. At times during that fateful year, it had felt as if the gods were bent on destroying all of them.

Only she and Tony had escaped. But then they'd had to run off into the mountains with Jeremy when she was ten and Tony thirteen to get away from the foster home.

She blinked until the sting of tears subsided, then slipped off her shoes and curled her feet under her while she looked through the magazine. A fleece throw felt good over her legs.

After a while, the words blurred. She laid the magazine aside and watched the wind toy with the fir branches at the corner of the house. One yawn followed another. She warned herself not to go to sleep, but her head sank back against the supportive wing on the sofa....

Lance sat in the leather chesterfield chair where he'd often sat as a child and listened to lectures from his grandfather on proper behavior for a Carrington.

The soft snores from the old man, who rested in his favorite recliner with a blanket tucked around him, assured him of his grandfather's immediate well-being. His breathing didn't seem labored at all.

Observing the thin, lined face, which appeared pale and drawn, Lance suddenly realized his only living relative wasn't indestructible.

Perhaps he'd thought the eighty-five-year-old man would live forever, like a vampire. That's what he'd thought when he'd come to live here twenty-five years ago.

His grandfather had seemed all-powerful, like a god...or a demon...who would rule his life forever.

But all things come to an end, the good and the bad. He'd gone off to college, then started his own business. He'd never looked back.

The door to the library opened silently. Morgan came in. He brought a tray with an insulated urn of coffee and a cup. "Would you like something to eat?" he asked, placing the tray on the side table.

Lance shook his head. He muttered a curse. "Krista hasn't had lunch. Would you fix something for her?"

"She's sleeping. Shall I awaken her?"

"No, let her sleep. She's been working long hours this month. And before that. I wanted this to be a relaxing day for her, but I didn't plan on boring her to death."

He and Morgan exchanged smiles, then looked at the other man in the chair as he snorted and mumbled in his sleep, words they couldn't understand, but it was obvious he was troubled in his dreams.

After the servant left, Lance poured a cup of coffee and studied his grandfather. Did he miss his wife? She'd been the one person the old man had always shown respect for…and tenderness. Lance had been shocked once upon walking into his grandmother's sitting room and finding them kissing. He hadn't known old people, especially his grandfather, did such things.

Smiling at the naiveté of his youth, he added another log to the dying fire and settled in the chair again, his gaze on the flames that leaped around the wood, his thoughts on Krista.

The softness of her lips during the ill-advised kiss, the smoothness of her skin against his hand— the memory returned to him, as fresh as if it had just occurred.

He'd wanted much more than kisses the instant he'd felt her mouth under his. The haunting power of the kiss had bedeviled his dreams for hours.

He was sure the attraction was mutual. And strong. He didn't blame her for running away from him. If she hadn't... He didn't think he could have let her go.

And that was damned foolish, as his grandfather had told him many times about his ideas.

Foolish, but so sweet, even the memory set his pulse to pounding. As longing rose in him, he realized that, for the first time, he needed something more.

Would he find his soul mate in Krista?

Some cynical part of him laughed, but another part wished he *could* believe in the possibility of happily ever after.

Krista turned from the window at the sound of footsteps in the hall. Lance entered the sitting room.

"I'm sorry to leave you alone so long," he said, coming over and standing beside her. They both looked at the gleam of late afternoon sunlight on the mountains and lawn.

"It's okay," she admitted. "I had a nice nap, then I read some magazines on landscaping. My family did a lot of gardening when I was a teenager, growing our own vegetables as well as flowers. I didn't realize how much I'd missed it until I saw your grandfather's lovely grounds." She glanced up at Lance. "How is he?"

The gray eyes flickered with emotions she couldn't read. He shrugged. "He seems okay. I got him to agree to go in for a complete checkup Monday."

"That's good."

"He's extended an invitation for an early dinner. Can you stay longer?"

"Of course."

"This isn't a command performance," he said with a sudden, fierce frown. "We don't have to accept."

"I don't mind staying. Besides, I'm hungry." Her smile was meant to ease the tension in him, but it didn't work.

He gazed at her face—her eyes, her lips, back to her eyes. There was a moody, restless anger about him. It didn't take a genius to know he and his grandfather didn't exactly hit it off.

Raising both hands, he gripped the ornate wood trim on each side of the window, his body no more than an inch from hers, his arm brushing her shoulder. She was aware of him in the most elementary particles of her being. Every breath he took, the slightest shift of his weight, the waves of heat radiating between them like a force field...

A heaviness developed inside her. She wanted to turn and snuggle into his arms, to have him surround her with his strength and passion. She wanted his kiss and his embrace. She wanted to touch and be touched. Everywhere.

"Wh-what time will we eat?" she managed to ask.

"Soon. Morgan's wife is preparing appetizers to tide us over until she gets dinner ready. We'll have those with some wine in the library."

"Great."

"Look at the sunset," Lance said softly.

She looked out the window at the fluffy white clouds that dotted the peaks. The sun was behind them and shining around the edges, making each one gold-rimmed.

"That's beautiful," she said in a near whisper.

"Yes," he murmured.

She felt his breath against her temple, then his lips were there. She couldn't breathe, couldn't think. Then she realized neither was necessary.

Leaning against his arm, she let herself revel in the soft touches of his lips along her cheek, down to her ear, then the side of her neck. His breath slipped under the softly draped neckline of her sweater and created a tempest of need that centered in her breasts.

She sensed her body heating up, her flesh softening, the liquid, sensual hunger preparing her for his touch.

Pushing her hair aside, he nuzzled every exposed inch of her neck and throat, leaving hot spots like tiny volcanic overflows on her skin. When he stepped closer, she leaned into him and felt the proof of his desire against her hip.

His arousal fed her own. It raced through her, leaving flushed, hot skin in its wake. When she trembled, he dropped his hands to her hips and rubbed very gently against her, increasing the heat between them.

She felt as if she'd stepped into a furnace. Worse, she didn't want to leave. She wanted to be consumed.

When he slid his hands over her abdomen, then down the front of her thighs and back to her waist, she became so lost in the red haze of desire she thought she might faint.

"Krista," he whispered.

Words flashed through her mind, but none made it to her lips. She leaned her head against his shoulder and turned her head slightly. His mouth slid over hers and lingered lightly, as if he wanted only a taste.

When she pressed upward, rising just a bit on her toes, he took the kiss deeper, harder. When he stroked across her lips, she opened to him and was rewarded with the sweet embrace of his tongue on hers.

His hands ran up and down her torso, as if to soothe the passion, but the effect was to drive it higher.

She wanted more. She wanted to fall upon the comfortable sofa where she'd slept for two hours and take the fulfillment she knew she would find with him. She wanted to give him the same—to ease the anger and tension and unhappiness she could feel inside him.

"Mmm," she said, a throaty sound that echoed the demand her body was making.

When he touched her breasts, she reacted with a sensuality that was purely instinctual. She arched to his caress and felt her breasts become hard with longing.

With an eagerness for contact she hadn't experienced in ages, she explored him, loving his warmth against her palms as she spread her hands on his thighs. The power in the flex of the muscles there thrilled her.

With a quick movement, he turned her to face him, then lifted her to the broad windowsill. He pushed against her and again she opened to him.

Both of them sucked in ragged breaths as an inferno raged between them at the intimate contact. The hard ridge of his erection stroked against her most sensitive place as he moved with light but insistent demand against her.

She wanted to shout, *Yes! Yes! Yes!*

But some tiny remnant of preservation kept the words locked inside. She didn't know what, besides the physical, he wanted from her.

The attraction was powerful. She would find sensual fulfillment, but would that be enough?

For him, probably.

For her?

The humiliation of the one time she'd been in love warned her that this man wasn't thinking of commitment and forever. If she fell in love with him… If she were that foolish…

She remembered the despair when she'd lost those she'd loved, the pain of rejection and the false promise of happiness.

"D-don't," she said, pulling away.

And just like that, he let her go and stepped back.

They stared at each other warily as the mists cleared from their eyes. She couldn't read his expression, but he seemed as shocked by the encounter as she was.

"My God," he murmured. Then he walked out and left her holding the window frame for support.

Chapter Seven

"This way to the library," Morgan said, taking a one step lead down the hall.

The last Krista had seen of Lance, he'd been striding across the lawn toward the line of cotton-wood trees, bright green in their spring finery, that lined the meandering path of a creek.

It was with some trepidation that she entered the large masculine room lined with books, its furniture dark wood or deep brown leather with brass tacks. It looked like an exclusive gentlemen's club to her.

A man, as tall as Lance and with the same gray eyes, stood at the hearth, gazing into the fire. He had solid white hair and a patrician face. He smiled in welcome when she and Morgan walked in.

"You must be Krista," he said and came forward to shake her hand and lead her to a chair. "My grandson tells me you're a whiz at finances."

The older man's hand felt dry and papery against hers. She smiled politely and took the seat he indicated. "I'm not nearly as proficient as Lance and Toby," she told him.

"Ah, yes, Tobias," Mr. Carrington murmured. "Those two are considered the über-team of today's corporate takeover."

Recalling the past two weeks, she said, "I agree."

While he took a seat in a leather recliner, Morgan served them each a glass of red wine. "A merlot," the servant told Krista.

"I drink one glass every night," Mr. Carrington said in a somewhat ironic tone. "The doctor says it's good for my heart."

She sipped the wine. It made her mouth water and reminded her she'd had no lunch. "You're wise to take care of yourself, sir."

She saw Morgan glance at his employer, then her, as if he might dispute her conclusion. Instead, he removed a plate from a mobile teacart and placed it on the side table next to her along with a linen napkin that enclosed a fruit knife and fork. Then he did the same for her host.

"Anything else, sir?" he asked.

"That will do." A scowl briefly appeared on the broad, refined forehead. "Did my grandson indicate when he would return and be so kind as to join us?"

Krista took umbrage at the undercurrent of sarcasm. A flash of guilt assailed her, then she reminded herself that the hunger had been mutual…and that she hadn't started the episode in the sitting room.

"I'm sorry, sir, he didn't."

"Fine. Perhaps he'll be here in time for dinner." The old man waved his hand in dismissal.

After Morgan replenished the logs in the fireplace, he left, closing the door after him. Krista waited until her host spread the napkin in his lap and pulled the plate closer to him before she did the same.

The fruit salad—melon balls, apples, kiwi and dried cranberries—had a light, lemony dressing and was served with crackers and a delicious cream cheese spread. When she looked up from her plate, Lance's grandfather was observing her rather pointedly.

"This is very good," she said. "I, uh, we didn't have lunch…"

That didn't sound very gracious, since it was obvious they'd come here instead of continuing on their trip.

"What do you think of the merger with CCS?" he asked.

She pressed the snowy napkin to her mouth before replying. "It saved our company from bankruptcy. We were on the brink of financial disaster. Lance, Toby and I are developing a plan to turn things around."

"What do you think of my grandson?"

His gray eyes seemed to penetrate right into her skull. She felt the blood rushing into her face, as if he could see the kiss that had taken place down the hall twenty minutes ago.

"He has a brilliant mind for business." There, that established the proper tone for this line of questioning.

Or inquisition.

She could almost see this same scene being enacted between Lance and his grandfather as the older man queried his every move. She wouldn't have liked that.

Neither would Lance.

Nor did she like being questioned about the absent grandson. What did Mr. Carrington think she was going to say about Lance that he didn't already know?

They ate in silence while the fire crackled in the grate and the late afternoon wind picked up, blowing down the mountain with a keening sound as it rounded the eaves of the four-square house.

Lance, she recalled, hadn't worn a jacket when he went outside to walk off the tension and, she assumed, the passion of their encounter.

Don't worry about him, she warned herself. He's a big boy; he can take care of himself.

Finished with the appetizer, Krista sipped the mellow wine and stared into the flames, her mind adrift in a haze that required no thinking and therefore no rationalization of unwise lapses of judgment.

Mr. Carrington ate only a few bites, then laid his fork down and also peered into the fire. "He's never forgiven me," he said in a low voice.

"I beg your pardon?" she said, not sure whether he was talking to her or thinking aloud.

"When he was a boy and came here to live, I refused to let him see his parents. I wanted to cut them out of his life the way a surgeon cuts out a tumor."

Krista kept a poker face, but she was shocked that the older man had wanted to cut his own son out of their lives.

He sighed, then sipped the wine, seemingly lost in his thoughts for several long minutes. Krista didn't add anything more.

"Later, after my son died, Lance wanted to bring his mother here. I refused."

Krista kept her eyes on the fire and didn't respond.

"My wife warned me," he said, also staring into the hearth, "but I didn't listen. I should have. A boy's love for his mother. I ignored that bond and how powerful it could be…and I broke his heart."

Tears burned the back of her eyes. The magazine article had said Lance was ten on the day the court gave him to his grandparents to raise.

Mr. Carrington gave a snort of bitter laughter. "I blamed her for my son's death. It wasn't until later, long after both he and my daughter-in-law were gone, that I learned the truth. My son indulged in a variety of ill habits in college and throughout his short life. He was the one who introduced alcohol to his wife."

She heard contempt in his words and realized it was for himself. "I'm terribly sorry, sir," Krista said sincerely.

"I was a self-righteous bastard out to save my grandson from his mother's sins...and pay her back for leading my son astray. What a fool," he finished, so softly it was as if he were talking to himself.

She had a feeling he'd often had this conversation with his conscience, alone in this room. As an interloper, so to speak, she didn't like being a convenient sounding board for the old man's remorse. It felt unfair to Lance.

"He begged me to help her," the soft voice continued. "He cried. I told him men don't cry."

Krista cringed internally. Lance had been ten years old, a child taken from his beloved parents. She knew how that hurt, how deeply a young soul could be injured...

"She died that winter. Of pneumonia."

"Sir, perhaps you should tell all this to Lance—"

"Impossible," he cut in. "He walks out if I even mention his parents."

His expression was one of the saddest she'd ever seen. She wondered if he thought he was dying, if this was a deathbed confession to purge his own sins. Glancing at the door, she wished Lance, or Morgan, would interrupt.

"He didn't cry when we went to claim the body," Mr. Carrington told her, his gaze harsh when he looked up. "He didn't cry at the funeral." He took a shaky breath. "He's never cried again in his life as far as I know."

"No, he wouldn't," she agreed.

The old man gazed into the fire as if the leaping flames reflected haunting images from the past. "He'll be thirty-five in a couple of months. He needs to take his mind off business, to settle down and have children. He needs to learn to love and trust another in order for his heart to be whole."

Krista clenched the glass stem so tightly she was afraid it would break off in her fingers. Not knowing what to say, she kept her eyes on the flames and wished to be anyplace but where she was. Lance would be furious if he knew his grandfather was speaking of him to a stranger—

"Telling my life history, Grandfather?" he asked, sweeping into the library with the fresh cold aura of the outdoors clinging to his tall, masculine frame. "Look, you've made Krista cry. Not a good thing to do to a guest, who probably wishes she were a thousand miles away."

"I'm not crying," she protested. She blinked and

realized there was moisture in her eyes. "Not for you, at any rate." But her heart ached for the boy he'd once been.

"For my grandfather? He doesn't need your tears. They don't move him at all. Isn't that right?"

She hated this raw, cynical side of him. But she also recognized it for what it was—the shield erected by a young boy whose only defense was to use anger to close himself off from the world that hurt him.

"A man needs a family," was all the older man said. He smiled at both of them, the charming host once more. "Ah, here's Morgan. Dinner must be ready."

He held out his arm to Krista and escorted her to the dining room next door. Lance followed behind them. Glancing back, she saw him run his hands through his hair to smooth the dark, wind-tousled strands.

After returning her look, he smiled and everything seemed okay again. In a surprisingly small dining room, he pulled out a chair and seated her on his grandfather's right. He took the chair across from her.

"This is the family dining room," he told her as she glanced around.

The ceiling was a sky scene of blue with wispy white clouds blowing across it. The walls were green, the intricate woodwork glossy white. Green velvet curtains framed the bay windows set with plantation shutters.

"It's lovely."

"This and the sitting room were my grand-mother's favorites." He gestured to an oil painting of a landscape with paths wandering among trees and flowers. "She loved the colors of nature. There are hundreds of pink tulips in the spring and masses of roses all summer."

"You must come back in a month when the spring bulbs will all be in bloom," his grandfather added.

The men made sure she was entertained during the meal, which started with a cup of asparagus soup, then a main dish of salmon baked in shrimp bisque with rice and roasted mixed vegetables. An hour later, they finished with ice cream and a chocolate-covered wafer.

"Please tell your wife that was a wonderful meal," she said to Morgan when he cleared the table and poured freshly brewed coffee into porcelain cups.

"I will, miss, and thank you," he said. He left the room by a different door than the one they'd entered.

"Morgan will bring you to town in the morning," Lance now told his relative. "I'll see you at the clinic."

"There's no need for you to take time off." The gray eyes, so like Lance's, glanced her way. "You two must have meetings scheduled."

"Toby can fill in for me until I get there."

Krista felt a sinking inside and realized how much she'd counted on Lance to lead the way and make things easy, or at least easier, for her at the board meeting.

"You don't have to do your duty toward me," his grandfather said in a querulous tone.

"I always do my duty," Lance said without a change of expression. "As you taught me, sir."

Monday morning, Toby picked Krista up at nine-thirty for the short journey to CCS headquarters. "Lance sends his apologies," the other man told her. "He says he'll see us at the office."

"No problem," she said coolly, but her spirits at once perked up at this news.

"I think he had to check on his grandfather," Toby continued, a worried frown on his face. When he caught her observing him, he smiled wickedly. "Maybe the old boy will kick off soon and Lance will be rid of him."

She managed not to appear scandalized at his flippant manner. "From seeing them together yesterday, I take it they don't get along."

"You sound somewhat shocked," he teased, whipping into a parking space at their destination. "Families don't always mesh, you know."

"I do know. My stepsister and her mom, who's married to my guardian, didn't get along at all while she was growing up. Since I thought they were both great, I hated that things were tense between them," she explained while they walked toward the parking elevator that would take them to the top floor of the building.

"Wouldn't your stepsister's mom be your step-mother?"

"Well, she's sort of my step-aunt, actually." Krista laughed as he obviously tried to put all this together. "Zia and I call each other 'sister,' but we're not really kin, except that her mother is married to my uncle, my step-uncle. He became my legal—"

"Guardian," Toby finished for her. "I get it. Lance told me a little about your past when he was explaining what a whiz you are at finance. He told me I'd better watch out for my position, that you're a go-getter."

They laughed easily, like old friends, as they stepped out of the elevator and into the lobby. She spotted Lance at once when they approached his office. He had some papers in his hands and was talking to his secretary, a middle-aged woman with prematurely gray hair.

Or maybe working for him aged a person, Krista thought, tension building in her as she and Toby spoke to the other two. Lance introduced her to the woman, then they all went into a conference room that could seat twenty people.

While she wondered about his grandfather, she felt it wasn't her place to ask. Lance would tell her what he wanted her to know. Right now, she'd stick to business. "How large is your board?"

"There are twelve of us, plus eight corporate officers. Toby and I are the only ones who serve on the board as well as hold positions as officers."

"President and treasurer," Toby told her.

"At Heymyer, James had only those officers required by law, plus me for finances. Is Toby acting as the third member of our corporate entity?"

Lance nodded. "For now. Since Heymyer is a wholly owned subsidiary of CCS, our board is the governing body and will have to approve the final slate of officers." He looked directly at her. "You've already been approved as the COO."

She nodded, understanding the position had come about on his word. She also knew the title was temporary, until new officers could be hired. Some headhunter might be searching for a new CEO at this moment.

And a new COO/CFO?

Some of her old insecurities crept back into her mind. When Lance told her to sit on his right at the big table, Krista took the chair and folded her hands together in her lap, aware of the slight tremor that would give her away.

She felt on display, like a prize pet at a dog show. Would she earn a blue ribbon from these judges?

The real question was, would she have a job when these six months were up?

Glancing up, she met Toby's blue eyes. He gave her a wink and a nod. With his blond curls and good looks, he seemed younger than Lance, more lighthearted.

Lance, she decided, was like her—serious and

focused on whatever problem was at hand. With his wealthy background, she'd wondered why he'd felt compelled to start his own business and pour so much of himself into it. Now she felt she knew.

He'd said that ten was an impressionable age, that some things were never forgotten. It hadn't occurred to her that he was referring to himself as well as her.

How much had he heard of his grandfather's tale before he'd entered the library? Would he resent her knowing about his past as much as he resented his relative for telling about it?

Her eyes went to his tall form near the open door of the room. He glanced at her. Flashes of emotion arced between them like electricity rushing from one pole to another, linking them in ways she couldn't describe. When the secretary spoke to him, he turned away.

As other people filed into the room, Krista forced her attention on them, rising and speaking cordially to Mr. Walters and Mr. Cookson, the two board members she'd already met. There were five women in the group, which pleased her.

After Lance called the meeting to order, she was formally introduced for the record. After getting through a short list of agenda items, the rest of the day was devoted to Heymyer Home Appliances.

The reports she'd prepared, along with the changes and notations she and Lance had worked so hard on, were neatly typed and arranged in a bound notebook with her name as the author. When she glanced at Lance, his smile was one of encouragement and confidence.

After having lunch served in another equally spacious room, they returned to the conference room. The new company names she put forth were thoroughly considered. The final decision was National Home Market, which would better reflect the company as it moved into other areas, such as personal grooming.

She answered every question, with Lance or Toby chiming in with additional explanations when necessary. At six that evening, they adjourned.

"You handled that very well," Toby told her with a broad grin on his way out.

After he left, she turned to Lance, hoping she didn't look as ragged around the edges as she felt.

"Toby put your suitcase in my car," he said with a brief smile at her, closing his briefcase. "Are you ready to head back to Grand Junction?"

Was she ever! "Yes," she said calmly.

They went down the elevator in silence. "Good night, Mr. Carrington," a security guard called out as they entered the parking garage.

"Hey, Johnny, how's it going?" Lance replied.

"Fine, sir."

"Do you know everyone who works here?" she asked as they continued to the car.

"Yes." He raised his dark, straight eyebrows at her look of surprise. "I should. It's my building."

"You own it?"

"I bought it as a fixer-upper several years ago. It was my first venture into real estate. Some people thought it was a mistake since the building was a white elephant on the market, but remodeling paid off."

"You had vision," she said, approval in her voice. "A person has to see the possibilities in order to succeed."

"Yeah," he said, his gaze intent upon her.

She looked away.

He stored the briefcase in his trunk with her one piece of luggage. He laid a hand on the back of her neck as he guided her to the passenger seat.

"You did very, very well today," he murmured, his breath fanning her temple as he leaned close and spoke in a soft, intimate tone.

Instead of getting inside, she stood there, smiling like a kid who'd just gotten an *A* from her favorite teacher.

His eyes narrowed, then he gave a low groan.

The next thing she knew, she was being kissed…very thoroughly kissed…so deeply kissed her knees started trembling. She leaned against the car, her left hand grasping at the door frame for dear life.

She couldn't breathe, couldn't think as blood rushed out of some secret place in a flood of desire.

Dropping her purse onto the car seat, she lifted her arms and wrapped them around his shoulders as the world went as hazy as her mind. Dear God, she wanted this.

Lance moved his head, tilting to the side as he took in the taste, the texture, of her lips like a starving man coming upon a feast in the desert.

Part of him, the older, wiser part that had learned to keep a careful eye on the world, warned him of danger.

Another part, the one that wanted to forget past lessons and future hurts, urged him on.

That part won out.

The passion rose higher and higher between them. He ran his hands down her sides, stopped at the alluring curve of her hips. When she ran her hands into his hair and caressed his neck, heat roared through him, a furnace of need and hunger he'd ignored for years.

Leaving her tempting lips, he roamed her face, her neck. A tiny pulse point in her throat beat like a trapped hummingbird against his lips.

She gave a tiny groan that spoke of passion long denied. Like him, he thought through the whirling mists that clouded rational thinking. Like him, she'd poured herself into other things and forgotten this part…this very enticing, very sensual part. Now they couldn't seem to keep it locked down tight.

Lights flashed across them.

Lance lifted his head from her neck and was blinded by headlights as another car left the garage.

"Damn," he muttered.

Looking at Krista, he saw she was watching him, wariness in her expression now.

"Let's go," he said, his voice still husky with unfulfilled desire. "We need to get on the road."

"Yes."

She slipped away from him, leaving a cold place where her body had touched his. He closed the passenger door while she was busy fastening the seat belt.

"Can you wait another forty minutes to eat?" he asked. "I know a good restaurant west of town, not far from the interstate, so it isn't out of the way."

"That would be fine." She paused, then asked in a level tone, "Friday night was due to a pleasant evening. Yesterday was probably due to tension. What do we chalk the kiss up to this time?"

"Good question," he told her.

Too bad he didn't have an answer.

To her amazement, Krista actually went to sleep on the long ride back to Grand Junction after dinner at a very nice steakhouse outside Denver. Lance walked her to the door when they arrived at her town house apartment. He set her suitcase over the threshold into the living room, but didn't go inside.

"I've been thinking," he said, his eyes searching

hers as she thanked him for the ride home. "I've never mixed business with pleasure, and I'm sure you haven't, either."

She nodded, a warning chord resounding through her.

"But there's an attraction here," he continued, his hands clasping her upper arms as if to keep her from running away. "What would happen if we acted on it?"

"We wouldn't," she quickly said, refusing to even consider it. "That would be foolish."

"Probably," he agreed, but his eyes were saying other things as they roamed her face. "But we're smart. If we kept emotion out of it—"

"Can that be done?" she asked. "A relationship based solely on passion?"

He stroked along her arms with his thumbs, causing sensation to pour over her. It had been so long since she'd felt this way—the inner tingling, the need to touch and to feel another person's caress, to know him nearly as well as she knew herself.

Dear God, it was so tempting. And so insane.

That he felt the same didn't make it any easier to hold her longing in check.

"There's respect," he murmured, frowning as if trying to work out the relationship in his mind. "We're logical…except there's nothing logical about this."

His rueful smile did those tingly things to her insides again. She managed a wry grimace. "I know.

I wonder if it isn't the intensity of work and how involved both of us are in this merger. That may build a sort of camaraderie…like soldiers in combat."

"Ah, I knew there was an explanation," he said, amusement deepening the laugh lines near his eyes.

She gave him a serious frown. "I think it's best if we keep strictly to business and forget the other."

"I'm sure you're right."

Then, to add to her conflicting emotions, he leaned forward and kissed her again—a whisper of a kiss—then he closed the door, made sure she locked it and headed off into the night.

She pressed her fingertips to her lips and wondered if they would succumb to the temptation.

Squeezing her eyes shut against images that were both foolish and wonderful, she feared the question wasn't *if* they would give in but *when*.

Chapter Eight

On Tuesday, Krista was reluctant to enter the conference room where Lance stood with an array of charts spread before him. Toby was there, too, having arrived on an early flight that morning.

After she finished a call to the head of contracts about the reasons the company had canceled, she joined the other two.

"What's bothering you?" Lance asked.

"Several things," she said. She explained about the call. "He said he was told to find another manufacturer because we couldn't meet the schedule we'd promised. He was under the impression we couldn't get the necessary parts."

"Did he say where the info came from?" Lance asked.

She shook her head. "He didn't know. The word came to him from the marketing VP, who happens to be out of the country for the rest of the month."

"Probably arranging foreign production while he's exploring their markets," Toby added.

She gave him a glum look.

Lance touched her shoulder in a brief, consoling manner. "We'll pull through," he told her, his tone totally confident.

Thea appeared at the door to the big office. "You have a call, Mr. Carrington. It's about your grandfather. Shall I take a message?"

"No, I'll take it. Thanks."

Krista was at once worried about the older man, but she didn't ask any questions as he headed for the door.

She picked up the production line flowchart. "Would you like to go out to the plant?" she asked Toby. "I want your opinion on another idea I have about standardizing some parts, which should result in a real cost savings."

"Let's go," he said, at once interested.

When she glanced over her shoulder at Lance, he was at his desk, watching them prepare to leave before he reached for the telephone. As she and Toby walked down the hall, she puzzled over the expression in his eyes. There had been encouragement and something more in those silvery depths.

Tenderness?

It was such an odd thought, she banished it from her mind and concentrated on the job at hand. For the rest of the day, other than a call to Marlyn at noon to postpone a luncheon date until dinner, Krista focused solely on company problems and put all personal ones on hold.

At one point in the late afternoon, she looked up from a cost analysis she and Toby were putting together. Lance stood in the doorway, his gaze on her. Their eyes met and held for a moment before he returned to the big office.

Heat rose inside her, driving all thoughts from her mind for a second. When Toby cleared his throat, she turned back to the sheets of figures in front of them.

"You would be *very* good for him," he murmured for her ears only.

"But would he be good for me?" she asked coolly.

At six, Lance declared it was time to quit.

"You want to join Toby and myself for dinner at the inn?" he asked Krista, his eyes on her.

She shook her head. "I ordered some takeout from the diner for me and Marlyn. Maybe I could join you for coffee in a couple of hours, though." She looked at Toby. "I have some questions on the cost analysis."

"Fine," Lance broke in. "We'll see you later."

Krista checked her watch as she jogged across the parking lot to her car. Time seemed to be getting away from her. All day she'd been on edge, constantly feeling she was falling behind. And she was.

Thea had forgotten to tell her that Lance had arranged a telephone conference with a couple of CCS engineers to discuss the changes she and Toby wanted to make. Tiff had finally run them down on the plant floor where they were doing a time-and-motion study on the new production line.

The conference had been lengthy and technical. She'd felt drained by the time it was over and she'd said good-night to her fellow workers.

Driving to the diner to pick up the food the owner had promised to have ready for her, Krista ruminated on the undercurrent of unease that had lurked in the back of her mind all afternoon.

She'd seen Mason talking to Thea after she had met with him shortly before lunch. She'd dreaded the meeting, in which she explained the new order of things. The CCS board had approved the new organizational chart, and Mason's title was now marketing manager.

She'd expected him to quit, but he'd been sanguine about accepting lower pay as well as the relocation to the desert. His attitude didn't jibe with her image of him.

Krista had often thought James let his son keep the New York office and gave him a stipend for living there just to keep him out of his hair. While there was a possessiveness in the older man's manner toward the younger one, there had been no apparent affection.

Odd, but she'd always felt sorry for Mason. Spoiled by his mother and relentlessly controlled by his father, he'd had a hard time finding his path through life. With the money he would get from the sale of his stock to CCS, she wondered why he didn't start a new life far from his father and a career he surely found stifling.

She gave a mental shrug. It was his business.

The meals were boxed and ready to go when Krista stopped by the diner. At Marlyn's house, she found her friend watching the local news.

"Nothing but murder and mayhem," her friend reported and hit the off button.

Marlyn got a couple of trays from the kitchen and laid out their dinners. "My favorite, spaghetti and meatballs. Thanks. This is a real treat."

After eating maybe half the meal, Marlyn set the tray aside and stared at the view out the window. Her house faced the mountains where Linc's work kept him. She sighed.

Krista prepared a teapot of hot cider and returned

to the other room with it and two mugs. "That cold front isn't moving through very fast," she commented, giving her friend a steaming mug and settling into the easy chair.

"I know. It snowed in the mountains over the weekend."

"Oh. We didn't get any around Denver."

Grand Junction couldn't claim to be a mile-high city as Denver did, but it was close. A few miles to the east, Leon Peak rose to almost twelve thousand feet. Somewhere between the town and the peak, Marlyn's husband worked on a dam that would form a new reservoir to supply water for the population boom around the ski area.

"It didn't snow any at this level. I drove up to the dam site over the weekend." Marlyn laughed, but it was a bitter sound. "The road wasn't the only thing throwing curves at me Saturday night."

Krista winced. "Was Linc with someone?"

"Yes, but not in the way you're thinking. He and the site secretary were playing cards with another couple in the construction trailer. I went there when I didn't find Linc in his RV."

"That sounds pretty innocent."

Her friend nodded. "I stood outside—it was sort of snowing and raining at the same time—and watched them having fun. Linc looked happy. Until he saw me staring in the window at them."

"What did he do?"

"I don't know. I got in my car and left. All the way down the mountain, I wondered how many nights he'd spent playing cards with *her* instead of coming home to *me*. While I endured the loneliness, he was enjoying a social life. I'd consoled myself that he was working hard to build a future for *us*. Except there isn't any us, not now."

"Marlyn—"

"Don't," her friend said softly, vehemently. "Don't defend him. It's over."

Krista sipped the hot cider, but its warmth didn't reach the icy spot. "Did he call?"

"Yes. I can't talk to him, not now."

Studying Marlyn's face, she sensed the other woman was holding herself together with the force of anger. She felt a terrible sorrow for her friend, but couldn't think of a way to make things better.

An hour later, Krista left the lovely home and headed for the inn. She and Toby had things to discuss. She forced herself to think of those and not the confused, unsettled way she felt inside when she thought of Lance.

Some bold, reckless part of her wanted to explore the passion between them. The part that disliked uncertainty and change sent out frantic warnings against it.

But, she reasoned, if she didn't expect more, if she grabbed the moment and simply enjoyed it, what would be so painful about that? As long as she didn't fall in love, all would be well.

Lance was waiting at the entrance when Krista arrived. He held out an arm to guide her up the steps and into a small, private dining room off the lobby. With her hand tucked into the crook of his elbow, she let his warmth and strength soothe her restless spirit.

After they were settled at the table with regular and decaffeinated coffee on the sideboard along with fruit, cheese and cream tarts, she and Toby went over the changes they wanted to make.

When they told Lance the cost savings they envisioned, he gave a low whistle. "You two are good."

At ten, Toby got a call on his cell phone. He bid them good-night and went to his room, his phone at his ear.

"Would you like something warm before you get on the road?" Lance asked her.

"How about a hot rum punch?"

He flicked her a questioning glance, then nodded and left. While he went to the bar located between the regular dining room and the enclosed terrace, she gazed out the windows at the softly lit grounds of the inn.

The heaviness descended on her spirits again. She agreed with Marlyn. The marriage was over.

"Why so glum?" Lance asked, returning with two steaming crystal mugs of elegant cut glass. "Are you worried about the changes?"

She shook her head. As he continued to gaze at her with a question in his eyes, she said, "It's my friend. She says her marriage is over."

"But?" Lance said, taking the seat beside her and moving closer.

"They've been in love since third grade. What happens to kill a love that's lasted that long?"

Their eyes met while they each took a drink of the hot punch. Steam swirled lightly between their faces, adding a mysterious air to the question.

"Indifference," he said. "Cruelty."

"Lack of priority," she added.

"As in?"

"Putting work above family. That's what Linc did. He never had time for his wife." She frowned. "I told her to talk to him, but when she went to him, he wasn't working. He was playing cards with a woman and another couple and having a good time."

"I see. That must have hurt your friend."

Krista nodded. "She doesn't want to see him or talk to him. She wants a divorce."

"It isn't your fault," he said softly.

"I was the one who urged her to make the trip."

He set the crystal mug down and lifted her downcast face with a finger under her chin. "Their problems are of their own making. People make choices."

"I care for them. I don't want either to be hurt."

"Sometimes," he said, a flash of some harder

emotion going through his eyes, "you can't kiss a wound and make it all better. It goes too deep."

She nodded, her gaze locked with his. "I know that. Sometimes you have to accept things as they are, not how you would like them to be."

For a second she thought she saw a sorrow in him that matched the pain inside her. Then he smiled slightly and rubbed across her lips with his thumb, stroking back and forth...back and forth...gently, so gently.

"It's a lesson I think you've learned well," he said in a tone so low she wouldn't have heard had they not been merely inches apart.

"And you," she said in a whisper.

"Yes, I learned it, too, probably around the same age you did."

A hint of cynicism invaded his voice, but not his eyes. There she recognized the lingering pain of long ago.

He'd lost his parents.

Like her.

He'd been sent to another place to live, a place he didn't want to go.

Like her.

She closed her eyes and tried not to feel pity for that young boy, or for the child she'd once been.

"Krista," he said.

The single word echoed inside her, shimmered

like a chimera that beckoned her to follow its path to…to what?

"Kiss me." She heard the voice and recognized it as her own, although she'd had no conscious thought of saying such a thing. She opened her eyes and gazed into his.

"I've wanted to. All day."

When he moved forward, she did, too. Her mouth met his. In that instant of touch, a flame leaped to life in the very center of her being, consuming her with need.

She wanted him. It was overpowering, to want this much. And a mistake. Emotions were unreliable.

It wasn't love, she reminded herself fiercely. She could handle the hunger, could take the passion…

As long as she remembered exactly what it was.

At some point, she felt his hands on her back, his palms directly against her skin. She inhaled deeply when they broke the kiss. Her breasts were heavy with desire.

He pulled back a little, causing her to moan.

"Krista," he said. "If I invited you to my room, would you come?"

She didn't even think about it. "Yes."

He expelled a gusty breath and removed his hands. He smoothed her sweater down, then clasped her face between his broad, gentle palms. "I've never wanted anything this bad, but it would be a mistake."

The words pulled her back from the brink of madness. She stared at him as sense began to return.

"You're not ready," he continued softly and planted a feathery trail of kisses from one corner of her mouth to the other.

She pulled away, settled back in the chair and picked up the mug of lukewarm punch, holding it with both hands to disguise her trembling.

"You're too emotionally involved with your friend's breakup," he told her. "I don't want you to come to me on the rebound from grief."

"Well," she said with a shaky laugh, "this isn't the first time I felt this way with you."

His smile was sweet and sexy and drove her right up the wall. She placed the mug on the table. She wished he *would* invite her to his room.

"The attraction is strong, but the timing is off. For now," he added, leaning over and feathering kisses along her jaw.

"Then don't kiss me anymore," she requested. "It makes it hard to think."

"I know, but it's equally difficult to stop. You taste delicious."

"The punch," she said.

"You," he corrected. He gave a low groan and slid his chair a good foot away from hers. "There. I've stopped."

"But now I don't want you to," she complained. "I don't understand myself anymore."

Their eyes met. They smiled at each other, wry smiles that spoke of unfulfilled hunger, but smiles nonetheless.

He stood. "I'll follow you to your place."

"You don't have to. I'll be fine."

Although he nodded, he escorted her to her car, then got in his sporty red vehicle and stayed close on the short trip across the river to her apartment complex.

"Flash your porch light twice to let me know you're safely inside," he told her, stopping behind her vehicle when she pulled into her parking space. "I'm not going to the door with you. I don't think my defenses are all that strong at the moment."

She considered inviting him in, then she admitted the insanity of the idea even as that reckless part of her demanded mindless bliss, no matter the consequences.

"Get out of here," a gruff masculine voice said. "Now!"

She rushed up the sidewalk, opened the apartment door, slammed it, then turned the porch light on and off two times. Then she stood there in the dark, panting like a small animal who had just escaped a mighty predator with her hide—and her heart?—barely intact.

* * *

Krista studied the calendar on her desk. It was Friday afternoon, the last workday of the month. Sunday was the last day of April. Where had the time gone?

It wasn't a facetious question. She truly didn't know. The days had passed in a blur of rapid changes she hadn't experienced since...since she was ten.

Lance had returned to the city to check on his grandfather, who'd had another spell of angina and was having more tests. The fact that he took time out of his busy schedule to look after his grandfather indicated he felt more for the older man than he admitted.

When his grandfather died, Lance would have no one. He would truly be alone. The loneliness of it caused an ache in her chest.

"Hey."

She looked up as Toby appeared at the conference room door. For the past ten days, including the weekend, she had worked with him for fourteen hours a day, going over all the finances.

"If there's nothing else on the agenda," he said, "then I'm off to the big city."

"There is one thing," she began, then stopped, knowing this was none of her business. "When I was in Denver, Mr. Carrington mentioned Lance's parents and that he'd refused to bring his mother home with them when Lance had asked him to. Mr. Carrington blamed her for his son's problems."

"His grandfather told you that?"

She nodded. "He knows he made a mistake. He said Lance won't listen when he tries to bring the subject up."

"Forgiveness isn't an easy thing for the Carrington men. When Lance's parents eloped while they were in college, the old man cut them off without a cent, but they made it through their last year without help. Lance was born a week after they graduated. With the family connections, Brandon got a job at a large brokerage firm. They lived pretty well for a few years. I think that's part of what Mr. Carrington couldn't take, that they didn't need him."

"I read the son died in a car crash. Was it really something else and the accident story was a cover-up?"

Toby shrugged. "There was a wreck, but an autopsy indicated he was DUI. Brandon had lost his job long before that. They were in precarious circumstances, then Carrington offered them a large settlement to let him have Lance. They refused."

Krista was indignant. "He didn't do so great a job raising his own son."

"That's what they told him. He hired detectives to gather evidence that they weren't fit parents. For nearly two years, Lance and his parents hid, living on the street when their money ran out."

"Lance lived on the street?" she asked, shocked.

Toby nodded. "In abandoned buildings mostly.

Lance took care of his folks when they needed it. He stole food, but he wouldn't bring them liquor." He paused. "He told me this one night during our first year in college. We'd had a big test that day and were relaxing with a couple of beers. It isn't something he normally talks about."

"No, it wouldn't be. I was uncomfortable listening to his grandfather, but now I understand the anger Lance feels toward him."

"Lance thought if his grandfather had helped, if his mother had gone into rehabilitation after Brandon died, she could have been saved."

"But she died, and Lance blames his grandfather."

"Right. Maybe Lance needs to come to terms with that. And get over it so he can move on with his life." Toby eyed her thoughtfully. "He's had a couple of close encounters, but he always pulls back when a relationship threatens to go too deep. Maybe it's time for him to let go and enjoy life." He hesitated. "Maybe it's time you did the same." He glanced at his watch. "Okay, enough. I'm really leaving this time." He headed for the door.

"Have a nice weekend," she told him.

"You, too. No work, you hear?"

She grinned at him as he left.

After Krista left instructions with her secretary in case Lance called from Denver, she drove across town to a much-needed spa appointment.

Upon entering the gated entrance of what seemed a large estate, she parked near a vine-covered walkway and hurried inside. Calls were not allowed, so she made sure her cell phone was off.

The receptionist greeted her by name and handed her a robe. Krista went into the changing room, letting the quiet of the place seep into her mind.

This was the one luxury she allowed herself, a time out for good behavior, so to speak. Every fourth Friday, she left the office early in the afternoon for the discreet spa.

There she relaxed in an herb wrap while she had a facial, followed by a full-body conditioning treatment. After a twenty-minute steam bath, she dozed while having a manicure and pedicure. Her hair was trimmed, if needed, and she got an hour-long massage that left her as limp as cooked spaghetti. After that, a cone of ice was rubbed over her neck and shoulder muscles, where tension often resided.

In view of the hectic month she'd spent, she felt the treatment was not only richly deserved, but desperately needed. Three hours later, she went home, relaxed, refreshed and restored.

Sort of. Her thoughts returned again and again to the information she'd learned on Lance's early life. It had been a lot harder than she'd ever imagined. No wonder he seemed older and more somber compared to Toby.

Don't, she warned the part of her that worried about other people's happiness. As with her friends and their problems, she couldn't help Lance and his grandfather. It wasn't her business.

Besides, she had a life of her own to figure out.

But all her sage advice didn't stop the ache inside her as she thought of that stouthearted little boy, determined to save his mother, begging for help, weeping for her.

Her own heart felt as if it was breaking as she envisioned how worried he must have been. And after her death, how lonely he must have felt in that big mansion.

For reasons too deep to explore, she pressed her face into the sofa pillow and cried. For all children who were hurt by life. For Lance.

For herself....

Chapter Nine

The ring of the phone woke Krista from a sound sleep on Sunday morning. "Hello," she said grumpily.

"Hello, yourself," a wryly amused voice said, one she recognized at once.

"Lance," she mumbled, trying to focus on the clock. "Did I miss a meeting or something?"

She hadn't slept well Friday night or last night. Unable to lie still, she'd sat up and watched an old movie on TV.

"No," he assured her. "I, uh, I'm heading up your way to look at some property. I wondered if you felt like taking a ride since our last outing didn't work out."

That had been two weeks ago. "How far are you from here?" she asked.

"About thirty miles."

"Okay, that should give me enough time to get myself together."

"Wear jeans," he advised. "And hiking shoes if you have them. We'll have to walk through some weeds and brambles."

"Right."

She dressed and ate her cereal in record time. Drinking a second cup of coffee while she waited, she contemplated the hard beat of her heart and wondered if this was a good idea. She was vulnerable where he was concerned.

But when he arrived in the SUV, she grabbed her jacket, purse and hiking boots and headed out the door, no matter that her heart was thumping like a bongo drum.

"Let's go," he said once she was buckled in and they were on their way.

She smiled when he did, but she really wanted to hold him, just hold him, for a long, long time. "Where are we going?"

"I bought some property a few miles up the Gunnison from the inn. We closed yesterday. I want to take a look at it again. I thought you could give me some ideas on remodeling the house."

"That's Marlyn's field. I could probably get you a good price from her, though."

"Ah, the good ol' girl network."

"Yeah, right."

They laughed, a companionable sound that only caused the ache inside her to deepen. She didn't know what was the matter with her. She'd been topsy-turvy all weekend.

He passed the inn and continued up the paved road for a few miles, then turned onto another one. The third one was in much worse repair than the other two.

Krista held on to the hand support above her head as the SUV rocked from side to side on the pitted surface. At a few places, she could see that it had once been paved. At present it needed a new roadbed.

"Sorry," he said as they hit a particularly rough patch of potholes. "The real estate guy said the old man who used to live here wouldn't repair the road. He didn't like visitors. I can identify with that."

She studied her host, aware of him in a thousand ways, knowing it was dangerous for her to be alone with him.

Knowing, she admitted, but unable to resist.

He was as attractive in casual clothing as in a business suit. Like her, he wore jeans. A blue oxford cloth shirt hung open over a white T-shirt. Ankle-high hiking books were on his feet.

"In the interview for your friend, his article said you lived in Denver," she mentioned.

"That's right, the penthouse above CCS headquarters."

Her mouth dropped open. "I didn't know that."

"Yeah. I try to keep business and pleasure on two different levels," he said wryly. He flicked her a quick glance. "It's always worked before."

She decided not to touch that line. "So why did you buy property out here?"

"I like the view of the mountains."

His answer was an evasion. "There's no place in Colorado that doesn't have a view of mountains. The one from your office of the eastern front of the Rockies is second to none. I repeat—why did you buy a rundown place in the middle of nowhere?"

"Maybe I needed a retreat."

"Maybe." Her tone was skeptical.

"Or maybe it suits me for business purposes."

"An investment?" That sounded more plausible.

He shrugged, but didn't say more as he navigated the nearly nonexistent road. It took over twenty minutes to traverse the five miles. Finally she spotted a house through some trees.

His grin was almost boyish when he stopped in a clearing. "Here it is. Home sweet home. A sanctuary from the demands of the world for the weary soul."

She rolled her eyes at his sardonic teasing, then surveyed the old homestead.

It was set back from the river and on high ground to be safe from flooding. A hundred or more years ago, some rancher had settled his family here and tried to make a living on this high desert plateau. The remains of a fruit orchard and flowerbeds dotted what had once been a broad lawn. Rock fences indicated where fields had been laid out for cultivation.

They sat there another few seconds, each lost in contemplation, until he said, "Let's look at the house. You'd better put on the hiking shoes. We might rouse some snakes."

While she changed from loafers to the sturdy boots, he got out of the SUV and came around to open the door.

"Watch it. That's poison oak." He pointed to a shrub close by. He took her hand as they stepped over a log.

She removed her hand from his clasp, much too aware of his warmth and masculine strength for her own comfort, and walked along a faint trail toward the two-story house nestled in deep shadow.

At the broad porch that faced the river, she stopped and looked over the old frontier Victorian. "The house needs a lot of repair. Some people would tear it down and start over with new."

"The foundation is good," he told her, again taking her hand as they went up the mostly rotten boards on the steps. "Some of the framing looks okay, but the rest will have to be replaced. The structure needs floors, drywall, modern plumbing and lighting."

"A big project," she told him. "Do you have a contractor yet?"

"No. I'm going to do a lot of it." His eyes seemed to light up at the prospect of the challenge.

"You?"

"I did some construction jobs during my college years. I like working with my hands."

"I suppose corporate raiders don't get to do that very often."

He paused and studied her for a second, his gaze deep and unreadable. She regretted the flippant remark, but before she could think of a way to mitigate it, he smiled and pushed open the front door.

She saw the framework had been ruined when someone broke into the place. "Well," she murmured, "you don't need the key. That saves time."

His chuckle did things to her insides. He held out the old-fashioned key, which was attached to a wooden key chain. "The carving is of the house after its last renovation over sixty years ago."

Krista took the key chain and perused the carving. The house looked solid and stately back in its heyday. A safe place to raise a family. Looking at it then, and now, caused an ache inside her. The abandoned home felt lonely to her.

"We have several very good architects in Grand Junction. A couple of them won national awards, which is impressive for a town of fifty thousand," she told him, mostly to distract herself from the emotional response she felt to the place. "Oh, but you'll probably use someone from Denver."

Some big city firm, she thought. Lots of prestige.

"I'm not sure I need an architect. I don't want to change the house, only rebuild what can't be saved."

She recalled the fun days of helping her foster uncle build a new, four-bedroom structure so Family Services would get off their backs. She'd loved working on their house.

Because it had been a family thing. She swallowed hard and wished she'd called and talked to her brother last night about how precarious she felt of late. Tony always understood her deepest insecurities.

"I thought men like you razed the structure and started over in their grand scheme of things." She didn't know why she said that. It wasn't what she thought at all.

He stopped in the middle of the spacious entrance hall that was a wide as her living room and ran the length of the first floor. "What kind of man do you think I am?"

One who grew from a hurt boy into an independent adult determined to keep emotion out of his life.

Her mouth went dry, but she managed a shrug.

"What a man does in the business world reflects what he does in life," he said in a low but hard tone. His eyes went wintry gray.

"I agree. If one runs ruthlessly over a company in a takeover, I suspect that person runs ruthlessly over other people in their personal life."

"You know this from experience?"

"Well, I—"

He had her there. The home appliance company was the only place she'd ever worked. She'd certainly never taken over a business and gotten it "back on track" as Lance had done several times.

Besides, so far—well, it had only been a month— there was no sign that he was going to raze their company.

"I'm sorry," she said, pushing her hands into her pockets. "I shouldn't have come. I'm not very good company this weekend." She sighed miserably.

"Are you still troubled about your friends?"

She managed a laugh. "About a lot of things."

He frowned, then said, "Let's see what's usable and what isn't. I didn't have a lot of time to inspect the house for ideas the last time I was here."

French doors with leaded glass were once used to close off the two rooms on either side of the hallway at the front of the house. They were still in good shape.

"What would you use these for?" he asked, gesturing to the two rooms.

She went into each and checked the architectural details. "This one was used as a library," she noted, pointing out the built-in bookcases on either side of the fireplace, which had marble insets around it. "The marble is cracked and chipped. That will need replacing, but I'd keep the room basically the same and use it as a library and maybe a home office."

"That's what I thought, too."

The ice left his eyes and he returned to the thoughtful and dynamic man she recognized. That tingly sensation rushed through her. Quickly, she turned and peered into the opposite room. "This was probably a formal parlor."

He glanced around the large room. "What would you do with it?"

"Actually I don't know. I've never had a parlor."

With a slight bow of his head at her quip, he took her arm and led her toward the back of the house. "The dining room," he announced.

It was a rather narrow room with a coped ceiling. An electrical box indicated the spot where a chandelier had once hung. The room had flocked wallpaper of dark burgundy.

"Ugh," she said, wrinkling her nose. "Pale cream walls above the wainscoting, I think. Lace curtains in summer, something elegant, velvet or silk brocade, for winter. Like your grandmother's dining room."

He studied the room for a moment as if considering her idea, then led her through a swinging door. "The kitchen."

"It's huge."

There was a screened porch on the side of the house. She checked it over, then stood in the doorway and considered it along with the kitchen. "This would be perfect for entertaining. By connecting this porch to the one that runs across the front of the house, you would have an excellent traffic flow for parties."

He opened one of two doors on the other side of the broad kitchen. "Bathroom."

She stood beside him and looked inside. "This would make a charming powder room."

"Mmm," he said in agreement. "I think this is a pantry." He opened the other door.

He moved aside so she could crowd in next to him. "Yes. I love all the shelves. That's the problem with modern apartments. They never provide enough storage."

When he didn't say anything, she glanced over her shoulder. His eyes were dark and mysterious in the dim light of the pantry. They were fastened on her.

She was instantly aware of several things. His chest against her arm. The warmth that surrounded them. The scent of balsam aftershave. The fact that they were miles from another soul.

Her throat clogged up. She swallowed and realized her mouth had gone dry, too. No words came to her to break the increasingly tense moment.

"You have thick hair," he murmured. He touched the wavy strands that she'd tried to blow-dry straight. "It shines so beautifully in the sun. I noticed it that first day, when I followed you into the parking lot." Lance shook his head to clear his mind. "Did you like your stepfather?"

She nodded. "He was fun and good to my brother and me. He followed the rodeo circuit, though, and my mother got tired of moving around. After they divorced, I missed him. He was the only father I ever knew."

"You've never heard from your biological father?"

"No. My brother, Tony, said he remembered our father and that he was a silent, irritable man with a temper, so I think it was better that he left. We were terribly poor after that, until Mom married again. Not that a cowboy makes a lot of money, but things were easier for a few years."

"Good."

His voice was muted, filled with the promise of good things to come. Like…passion?

They were still standing in the doorway to the pantry. It was an intimate space, and she realized they were speaking almost in whispers.

"Well, shall we check the rest of the house?" she asked on a louder note, giving him a bright-eyed glance as if eager to get on with the tour.

He stood aside and let her escape.

Lance was not the man she should be attracted to, she reminded herself. In fact, she couldn't make a worse choice. She was as stolid as a mountain, needing a firm foundation and eternity. He wanted none of those things.

She sighed, only realizing afterward that it had been a loud, gusty sigh, one of disappointment. He gazed at her with a question in his eyes.

Ignoring him, she went to the staircase, which was located in an open area opposite the dining room. The stairs creaked with each step they took.

The second floor had one old-fashioned bathroom, two large bedrooms and four small ones.

"What would you do up here?" he asked.

"Take out walls," she promptly answered. "I'd make one side the master suite with a private bath and dressing area. With a connecting door, this small bedroom would be perfect for a nursery—"

She stopped abruptly and gave him a quick, covert study. He went to the window of the large corner room and stared out toward the river, lost in thought.

Was he thinking of setting up his home, complete with wife and baby-makes-three?

Her heart and lungs suddenly felt too large for her chest. Don't go all emotional, she warned, knowing it was too late. She knew too much about him. He knew too much about her. And they were already involved, whether they wanted to be or not.

"I think I would consider leaving the wooden ceiling, but I'd paint it off-white," she said, recalling them to the moment. She headed across the hallway, which was narrower than the one downstairs. "You need a bathroom on this side, but otherwise leave the bedrooms intact. They're charming and plenty big enough for guests. Or children."

He nodded but didn't speak.

"The kids could have the smaller bedrooms. That way, you could keep the large one for your guests." She knew she should shut up. A man bent on an unemotional affair wouldn't be thinking of a family.

"What about closets? These seem rather small."

"Use armoires and/or dressers in each room to supplement the closets."

He nodded. "That sounds practical."

Somehow they were standing chest to shoulder again, her in front of him, peering in the large bedroom on the south side of the house. Her boots seemed pinned to the spot.

Looking up at him, she saw his eyes were fixed on some internal vision although he was staring at her. There was sadness and yearning in those depths. She felt it, too, a hunger for something more in her life, something more than an apartment that was used only for its quiet so she could go over business reports.

Recalling the laughter, the love that had made her feel so very safe in the Aquilon home during her teenage years, she wanted that feeling again.

"Ready to go?"

Krista nodded. Retreating down the steps, she decided she was mistaken about the emotion she'd seen. He'd probably been thinking of a business venture. With ten acres, he could put in a hotel or resort on the land.

"A resort with fishing guides, and hunting guides, too, would probably be a big draw for your corporate friends," she told him. "If you're thinking along those lines."

He gave a noncommittal grunt. When they were on the front porch, he closed the thick oak door and turned to the river once more.

"You like the river," she said.

He flicked her a glance, then turned back to the lovely scenery. "Yes."

She stayed silent when he didn't say any more. Instead she observed the sparkle of the sunlight on the surface of the water and listened to the now loud, now soft murmur as it flowed over and around rocks and the islands that dotted the river in this area.

A bird gliding across the yard brought her attention to the trills and songs that permeated the air around them. It was as if they were in an enchanted forest.

An ache throbbed to life inside her. She hurt and

she couldn't say exactly why, except that it was part of the yearning inside her.

After clearing her throat, she suggested they should go. "It'll be well past noon before we get back to town."

"I brought lunch. I wanted to explore along the river before leaving. There's a path along the edge. Actually it's more of a game trail."

She thought she'd been there long enough, but it didn't seem fair to insist that they leave, although she knew he would if she asked.

"Wait here," he told her and headed toward the SUV through the thigh-high weeds and grasses. She sat on the porch, her feet resting on an unbroken section of step.

In a minute, he returned with bottled water, thick ham sandwiches, two apples and four of the oatmeal-pecan cookies the Rosevale Grand was known for.

"The inn packs a nice lunch," she said, accepting her portion. She took a long, cooling drink of water. "They're used to guests going for hikes and day trips on the river, so they provide a hefty lunch."

"Yeah."

He ate in quick, efficient bites, his restless gaze moving from place to place on the land and river.

"Are you going to build a resort here?" she asked.

He frowned at her. "What makes you think that?"

His tone was intimidating, but she didn't flinch.

"The way you're assessing the site, as if looking at all the possibilities it offers."

He touched her temple with the tip of his index finger. "You're thinking all the time, aren't you?"

"You aren't answering the question."

"I don't know," he admitted. "It depends."

She wanted to ask "on what?" but figured she'd already used up her quota of questions. Munching on the delicious sandwich with its tangy hot mustard sauce, she considered her own future. Maybe it was time to move on. She glanced at the man sitting a couple of feet from her. She would miss him…

"Ready to explore?" he asked when she finished the lunch. He held out a hand.

She let him pull her to her feet. Together they set off on their grand adventure.

Krista followed Lance on the narrow trail that wound in and out of the woods along the riverbank. A short hike brought them to a semicircular cove of deeper, calmer water and a pier, which was in pretty good shape.

To her right, she spotted a cabin, a dilapidated structure that looked ready to collapse.

"I want to keep the pier," he said, "but I'm not sure about the fishing hut."

They veered off the path and waded through thigh-high weeds to the two-room unpainted building. The floor had completely fallen in, and the rock foundation at one corner was crumbling, a fact that caused the cabin to list to that side in a manner she thought precarious.

"Shows you how important a firm foundation is, doesn't it?" he said with a rueful expression as he checked the cracks in the foundation mortar. "Careful there. That beam has termite damage and might break."

He stepped outside on the flat rock that served as a step into the cottage and held out a hand to help her navigate the damaged structural beam.

As soon as she was on the rock, but not so fast it looked as if she was avoiding his touch, she let go.

Touching him did chaotic things to her inner being—like getting her all hot and tingly and wondering what he would be like as a lover. The hunger he induced couldn't be good for her peace of mind, although it might be wonderful if she but considered the physical side of it.

On the way back to the pier, he said, "There's a lot of poison oak around here. I'll have it sprayed out."

"Bring in goats. They eat it with impunity."

"Yeah?"

"My uncle cleared out a whole patch on our ranch in one summer. The goats ate it and some kind of invasive grass down to the roots. He staked them out on a long rope in the places he wanted them to eat."

"Aren't goats prone to butting people?"

She laughed. "Sometimes. Get pigmy ones. They're easier to handle. Some ranchers lease them out."

"Thanks. I'll consider your advice."

A smile touched the corners of his mouth as he gave her a wry glance. They walked out on the pier. The breeze from the river flowed over her face, pleasantly cool and bringing a hint of sage with it. He continued to the end of the solid structure. When he sat down and let his legs dangle over the water, she did the same.

The wood had weathered to a silvery gray patina and was surprisingly splinter free. The posts that anchored it to the bottom of the river were well over a foot in diameter.

"It's sturdy," she commented.

"It's made of Osage orange and an imported hardwood." He shook his head. "It must have cost a fortune."

"Perhaps a logging baron owned it at one time, or a banker. These old places are being snapped up as second homes these days."

With covert glances, she studied him. Maybe he did need a retreat from harsh reality. Here he seemed to find peace within himself as he quietly enjoyed the scenery.

She had to admit she did, too. The sun was warm on her back, the breeze cool on her face. The river murmured a lullaby like a mother humming a child to sleep. A yawn reminded her of the restless night she'd had.

"Fish," he said in a barely audible voice, pointing to a spot in the shadows near the edge.

She stared in the direction he pointed.

He leaned closer, his shoulder touching hers. "Over there, just to the right of that tree root sticking up."

The fish swished its tail and leisurely moved a couple of inches. "I see it," she whispered. "Do you wish you had a fishing pole?"

"Nah. I'm too lazy to want to do that much work today."

His grin caused her to smile, too.

She felt his breath fan her cheek as he stared at the tiny indentations near her mouth, then gazed into her eyes. Her smile faltered and withered away.

"Now you look serious. You've closed yourself off. Why is that?"

"Self-preservation." Being flippant didn't stop her blood from rushing madly so that it seemed the river had changed its course and flowed right through her.

"Odd, you meet someone and you start having thoughts about them," he admitted. "You stir an irresistible urge—"

"Resist it," she advised, making her tone firm and narrowing her eyes in warning.

"Can we?" His laughter was rueful and directed at himself as much as her. "Last night I kept thinking about us. If we kissed now, one taste wouldn't be enough," he said, staring at her lips as if only the thinnest silk thread held him back from taking that taste. "I'd want more from you."

She shook her head stubbornly.

He stood and held out his hand. "We need to be getting back."

She stood without help and headed for the path that would take them to the SUV and civilization. She was aware of him at her back, a predator—

No, she didn't think of him that way. She knew him too well. He wasn't ruthless, just very capable. But once, he'd been young and vulnerable, she mused, and he'd loved someone with all his heart. Longing rose in her as she contemplated the woman lucky enough to claim him. She would be loved completely—and forever.

Chapter Ten

Back at her apartment, Lance walked Krista to the door. There she turned to him. "Thank you for the trip and lunch. I enjoyed both."

The stilted manner was at odds with what he saw in her eyes. She wasn't as experienced as other women he had known. Her emotions lay closer to the surface. He recognized the hunger, the longing she couldn't quite hide. It matched what he felt inside.

He touched his fingers to her neck and stroked the smooth skin of her jaw. "Ask me in," he murmured, unable to hold the words back.

Her smile was quick, accepting. She'd known

all along what was likely to happen between them, he realized.

She unlocked the door, entered, then stood back so he could do the same.

As he stepped over the threshold, he took in the entrance area with its tiled floor, an office with French doors to his left and a large, pleasant living room to the right. The fireplace had a stack of pinecones on the grate. It looked as if it had never been used.

"There're two bedrooms and two baths down the hall," she told him. "That's the kitchen. The dining room is across the hall from it."

The kitchen had granite counters and stainless steel appliances. An island with a glass cooktop separated it from the living room, making the whole into a modern entertainment space.

"Nice," he said.

She placed her purse on a side table and stored her shoes and jacket in a closet. He slipped his boots off, too, and left them beside hers.

When she went into the kitchen, he followed and observed as she put the ingredients in the coffeemaker, the same top model her old boss had in his office.

"If you would like to wash up," she told him, "the guest bathroom is this way."

After finishing in the bathroom, he stood in the hall and glanced at the bedrooms. The guestroom was sparse. It contained a daybed, one side table and lamp, plus a chair, floor lamp and higher table with several magazines on it.

Her room held a queen-size bed with a pink, beige and green comforter in a floral pattern. The curtains matched. They framed a window seat with a green and beige plaid pad and several throw pillows. Pleated shades offered privacy from the side lawn. A chest of drawers with a mirror over it was the other large piece of furniture.

A bench at the end of the bed was covered in a beige chenille fabric. A bedside table held only a lamp and an alarm clock. No clothing was tossed carelessly on the bench or the floor. The intimate room had an almost impersonal look, like a hotel room.

Like his own place.

His eyes met hers as she crossed the bedroom and stood in the doorway. "Welcome to my humble abode," she said with a smile.

"The colors." He nodded toward the room. "They're similar to the ones in my grandmother's sitting room."

"I noticed that while I was there. I find the spring colors relaxing."

He had to smile. He didn't feel at all restful at the moment. Neither did she. When she brushed her hair behind her ear, he noticed the faintest tremor in her fingers.

Before she could drop her hand, he took it in his. "Don't be nervous. Not around me."

"I'm not." She tilted her chin upward and dared him to contradict her.

"Brave Krista," he murmured. "I'm nervous around you."

Her eyes opened wide at his confession. "Why?"

"Because." He stepped closer, unable to keep distance between them. "Because I want to touch you. Like this."

He slid his fingertips along her cheek, cupped her chin. With his thumb, he traced the outline of her lips, admiring the fullness on the bottom, the delicate curve of the upper lip.

When she opened her lips to take in a hard breath, he couldn't resist any longer. Leaning forward, he set his mouth against hers and felt a jolt clear down his spine.

Her response was immediate. And it wasn't enough.

He wanted more from her. This time they weren't going to be able to stop at kisses. When he stepped forward, she did, too. When he wrapped his arms around her, she did the same to him.

Her body molded to his, and his blood surged at the feel of her breasts pressing snugly against his chest. The hunger grew, the need to feel her close and naked, skin on skin, too strong to deny.

He lifted her and walked into the bedroom. She

swung her legs up and around his hips, clinging to him in a sweet, feminine bundle that clogged his mind with desire.

Stopping at the bed, he wondered if he should ask permission to settle there with her. Raising his head, he looked into her eyes and saw the answer he wanted.

With one hand, she swept the comforter over the footboard. He laughed at the impatient gesture.

"A woman after my own heart," he murmured, bending his head forward to taste those tantalizing lips again.

She turned her head slightly so that his kiss landed at the spot where the tiny dimples sometimes appeared. "Hearts don't enter into it," she told him in a low, fierce voice. "Only the moment and what we feel *now*."

"Yeah," he said and claimed her lips.

Krista forced herself to believe the words of wisdom she'd spoken. This moment, she thought. Grab the moment.

She let her hands run over his back, loving the flex of hard muscle and sinew under her palms. Loving the feel of him against her. The hardness of his passion. The gentleness of his hands. The fire in his kisses.

Oh, yes, she wanted this…so much she ached with the fierceness of the hunger.

"I want you," she said. "Now."

He set her on her feet, his hands going to the hem of her sweater. She held her arms up and let him slip it over her head. He tossed it to the bench. She did the same to his crewneck T-shirt, then followed the action by rubbing her hands over his chest.

Lance laid his hands on the flare of her hips and let himself enjoy the tactile sense of her hands running over him. She stroked her fingers through the thicker patch of hair in the middle of his chest, then trailed downward with one finger until she reached the snap on his jeans.

Glancing at him as if seeking permission—as if he was going to object!—she unfastened the snap, then the zipper.

Smiling, he did the same with her, then hooked his thumbs into the waistband and slowly slid the denim down her hips, her thighs, over her shapely calves. She stepped out of them when he reached her ankles.

Her nipples were beaded under the pink lacy bra, which matched the high-cut briefs she wore.

"Beautiful," he murmured, bending to tease one hardened tip with his lips, then his tongue.

She tugged at his pants.

He slid them down and off, leaving them in a puddle on the floor beside her jeans. The rest of their clothing followed as quickly. With one hand he pulled the pink blanket and floral sheet down while their lips met in another passionate kiss.

She was as he'd known she would be—all fire and flash, smooth and glittering, like a finely polished gem.

Krista reveled in the masculine feel of him, the hard skeins of muscle and sinew that lay under the skin. She liked the way the wiry hair on his thighs and chest felt against her, and the smoother flesh of his sides and back.

When she trembled, he placed one knee on the bed and lifted her onto the mattress. They came together in a tangle of arms and legs, their mouths eager on each other.

He kissed her neck, throat, paid lavish attention to her breasts, then tickled her belly button with his tongue, making her writhe and gasp with laughter. Then he slid lower, this time making her gasp with added hunger as he tasted and teased her body into the most intense passion she'd ever known.

"Come to me," she urged, frantic for more.

"I will," he promised.

"Now," she demanded.

"One second."

He moved away from her, then deposited three packets on the bedside table. She couldn't tear her gaze away as he ripped open a packet and prepared the protection before returning to her.

She opened to him as he settled between her thighs and began the slow journey that would make them one.

"Lance," she said on a quickly drawn breath. "Yes. Oh, yes. Yes."

He glided into the smooth, hot welcome of her

body and experienced the oddest sensation of intense excitement and peace…no, a sense of coming home after a long, long journey.

He rode her deeply and urgently as she bucked against him, her little cries driving him higher, further than he'd ever let himself go with anyone.

When she wrapped those long, slender legs around his hips, when she pulled him closer, deeper, when she cried out in pleasure, he went over the edge, not falling but whirling off into some sweet place he'd never known.

And after, while they rested in each other's arms, he realized he'd never felt this depth of fulfillment…and somehow, he knew there might be more…there could be more between them….

Krista had no idea how long she drifted in a lovely sea of contentment after they made love. She liked where she was—half lying on Lance, his arms around her.

"It's dark," he said. "After eight."

"I really did go to sleep." She didn't quite believe it, but glancing at the window shade, she realized the sun had set long ago.

He toyed with a lock of her hair. "And snored like a longshoreman."

She pushed herself up on an elbow and glared at him. "I did not. You take that back."

"Make me," he challenged.

They engaged in a tussle that invoked laughter, then soft chuckles, then quickened breaths as the hunger rose between them once more.

It was like the first time, only better, she thought, slower and more satisfying. Instead of a mad rush to the completion their bodies had demanded, they took time to explore more fully, to find a deeper delight in pleasing each other.

When she pushed him on his back and did all the things to him that he'd done earlier to her, he told her, "I like a forceful woman."

"Be still or I'll be *forced* to tie you up," she threatened when he thrust deeply into her.

They smiled, their eyes locked in a visual caress. Then he rolled her to her back and rested with his weight on his elbows. "Now who has the upper hand?"

But she didn't answer. His lips were on hers, and all the magic was there once more, lifting her…both of them…until she exploded in ecstasy and gave a little scream of completion. His groan immediately followed.

Later, dressed and calm again, she scrambled eggs with cheese while he toasted bread. "Your fridge is as empty as mine," he said.

"I don't cook very often. I eat a lot of salads in summer or soup in winter for dinner. And ice cream. I love ice cream with fruit."

"My mother's favorite was ice cream with strawberries and—"

When he stopped abruptly, Krista glanced his way. His lips were pressed together as if he realized he'd given too much away. She wanted to comfort that boy who had been taken into a world of riches but had lost those who mattered the most to him.

After they were seated at the table, she studied him covertly while they ate. The tension was back, indicated by two tiny lines etched between his eyebrows. It occurred to her that it could be concern for his only living relative.

Over fresh coffee, she debated with herself about mentioning his family. Becoming lovers didn't give either of them any extra privileges to pry into the other's life.

"How did your grandfather do on his tests?" she finally asked.

"Actually quite well. As long as he takes his meds and keeps the nitro handy for angina pain, he should live another twenty years." His chuckle was amused rather than bitter. "I'm not sure I'll make it that long."

"He spoke of your mother. When you were out walking."

A muscle ticked in his jaw as his face went hard.

"He's sorry he didn't help her," she continued. "He said he broke your heart by not taking her in."

"My grandfather reminds me of a man who drinks, gambles and runs around most of his life, then sees the evil of his ways and tries to tell everyone else how to live. It's easy to regret past mistakes when it's too late to change them."

"Your mother—"

He stood, pushing the chair back so that it squealed as it slid over the tiles. "She died broke and alone, without another soul knowing or caring."

Krista went to him and laid a hand on his arm. "Someone cared," she said softly. "A ten-year-old boy cared. He loved her with all his heart. She knew that, and that knowledge must have warmed the innermost places of her soul."

Lance turned his back on her. "But that love couldn't save her. It didn't change one single solitary thing about her life."

Krista wrapped herself around him, refusing to let go when he would have moved away. "No child could," she consoled him. "But as a man, you can forgive those who hurt you in the past. I think your grandfather needs that."

He loosened her hands but didn't push her away. Instead he pivoted, caught her in his arms and murmured fiercely, "I don't want to talk about the past. There's the here and now, and it's the best I've ever known."

His lips took hers in a long, hard kiss that shut her

up. She didn't fight him, but again wrapped him—the boy he'd been and the man that he'd grown into—in the warmth of her arms, needing to hold him.

She held him and kissed him and caressed him as he did her, until they again had to satisfy the great, passionate hunger they stirred in each other.

On Monday, Lance showered in the guest bathroom while Krista used the master suite. Time had a way of getting lost when they were close. And unclothed.

She smiled as she finished blow-drying her hair, then frowned as she dressed in tan slacks and a blue and tan blouse with a coordinating vest. She was going to have to sit down and think about yesterday and the situation between them at some point, but not yet.

"Are you coming to the office?" she asked, joining him in the kitchen. He was dressed in fresh jeans and a white T-shirt which he'd brought in a weekend bag.

"No. I need to get back to Denver. And you need to get to work. I've heard your boss is a curmudgeon."

He seemed relaxed and in a good mood this morning as he teased her. She hadn't mentioned his grandfather again, but perhaps he would think about the old man on the trip and decide to forgive the past.

After they left the apartment, he kissed her lightly

at her car, then touched the tiny frown lines that formed when she was worried. "We can handle this," he told her, his face solemn as his gaze delved deeply into hers.

She nodded, but she wasn't as confident as he was. "I don't want what's happened between us personally to spill over into the office."

"I agree," he promised, a devilish light coming into his eyes. "I'll think only of, hmm, mergers and interesting things like that."

She had to smile at his teasing. "You'd better think of balance sheets and where we're going to get the money for all your grand schemes."

"That's your and Toby's department. Keep that cash flowing," he ordered, then chuckled as he bent to her lips once more. "I'll see you later this week, probably Friday."

She nodded and they went their separate ways, she to the office while he headed for Denver. By the time she was seated at her desk, she missed him. Badly.

Going into his office, she sat in the executive chair that felt solid and steady. It was as if his arms were holding her securely in a welcoming embrace.

Last night, when she'd worried about their relationship at work, he'd told her she was the head of the appliance company and therefore her own boss.

"You're the CEO and the person I report to," she'd reminded him. "If a woman becomes involved with her boss, everyone assumes she's sleeping her way to the top."

"The same happens to men." At her skeptical glance, he'd continued. "If a man makes it to the top and seems interested in a woman, people say he sleeps with everyone in skirts at the company."

She'd given him a troubled stare. "That's hardly the same thing."

He'd shrugged. "I'm only the temporary CEO. NHM is its own company and you're the chief officer. If anyone gives you any trouble over us or anything else, you'll handle it."

She wished she had his faith in her ability to "handle" things. Truthfully, she'd never quite mastered the art of juggling a personal life in addition to the other duties.

At five-thirty on Thursday, Krista was still at work. Going over the plant operations with two industrial engineers from CCS and the three appliance design engineers had given her several insights on production flow, plus ideas for adding personal items such as electric shavers, toothbrushes and hairdryers to their products.

The phone rang. She saw it was the private line and picked up, her heart doing its usual thump-th-thump routine when Lance called.

"Hi," he said before she could speak.

"Hi. What's up?"

"How did the walk-through go?"

"Fine. We discussed some new ideas that I'll run by you when you get back." She hesitated. "There's one other thing that worries me. We had another order canceled this week, a standing order from one of our steadiest customers. Mason says the company is in difficulties and is cutting back."

There was a brief silence. "You don't believe him?"

"I don't know…and that bothers me."

"Do you have any contacts there?"

"I met their CFO at a seminar last fall."

"Call him. That's what networking is all about."

"I thought that was to find a new job."

"Don't even think of leaving," he warned in a mock fierce growl. "You have five more months per our agreement. I intend to hold you to it."

"Right."

She made a face at the phone after they hung up. Okay, she'd said no crossing of business with pleasure, and he hadn't. Not once during the week had he said anything that would even hint at the personal. But did he have to take her quite so literally?

The phone rang again.

Frowning, she lifted the receiver.

"Okay if I come over tomorrow evening?" he asked in a much different tone than the previous call.

Joy leaped through her as she realized he was,

as promised, separating businss from pleasure even in their phone calls. "Yes. Will you be here in time for dinner?"

"Probably not—maybe we can grab a late bite somewhere?"

"I think we can find a place."

When she hung up, she wrapped her arms around herself and held on until she could breathe easily once more, so glad he would be with her for the weekend. And so afraid she was in over her head.

Lance was glad to have cruise control on the trip to Grand Junction, or else he would have gotten a speeding ticket. Okay, he was in a hurry. What man wouldn't be when he was going to see a woman like Krista?

He'd missed her that week in spite of talking to her on the phone at least once a day. He'd kept the conversation strictly business, but at times it had been hard. He'd wanted to ask her personal things, such as—did she miss him as much as he did her?

In a few more minutes, he could hold her in his arms. They had the whole weekend to themselves. To be together.

He rotated his shoulders and tried to relax, but the anticipation that had been building since he'd started the trip wouldn't let up. At the apartment complex, he parked in visitor parking, grabbed his weekend bag and bolted up the sidewalk. The eagerness worried him for about five seconds.

"Hi," she said, opening the door before he could ring the bell.

"Hello," he murmured, hardly able to speak, his heart was beating so hard.

When he swept her into his arms, when their mouths were firmly locked together, the earlier tension went out of him, only to be replaced by the hum of desire now that she was finally in his arms.

"Mmm-mmm," she said, making little crooning sounds. When he released her, she gave him a dazzling smile and looked over his suit pants and white shirt. "Did you bring jeans? I want to take you to my favorite honky-tonk for some good food and real Western dancing. Are you up for it?"

"I'm with you, babe," he said, giving her a once-over and liking what he saw.

She wore tight jeans that showed off the smooth curve of her hips and her long, shapely legs. Cowboy boots added an extra inch or so to her height. The Western-style shirt wrapped around her torso like a second skin. The outline of her breasts was too tempting.

He bent and kissed each tip. "Whose idea was it to go out tonight?" he grumbled.

"Yours, cowboy, now change clothes and let's go, or I'll round up a posse to give you some grief."

"I think you can do that on your own," he grumbled, heading for the bedroom with his bag. There, he changed to faded jeans and pulled a chamois shirt over his T-shirt. His casual-Friday loafers would have to do since he'd brought only hiking boots for his spare shoes.

The place she directed him to was across town from where she lived. The music could be felt through the boards of the old building as they approached the front door. Inside, it was noisy, but dim and intimate.

A five-piece band played from a raised stage, the music blaring through oversize speakers as the couples crowded onto the dance floor. He hadn't been to a place like this since his college days when he and Toby used to prowl the bars, looking for girls or trouble, whichever came first.

After finding a table and ordering drinks and a platter of nachos, Krista glanced at him, then toward the dance floor.

"I'm game," he told her.

They squeezed in and joined the mob in a two-step, circling the floor twice before the number came to an end and the band segued into a love song.

"Ah, much better," he murmured, pulling her into an embrace. All her curves fit against him quite nicely. His pulse leaped into overdrive, and he was unable to conceal his reaction as he held her close.

It was after one when they returned to her place.

"Did you like honky-tonking?" she asked. "That's what everyone did on Friday nights when Marlyn and I were on the work/study program at the plant."

"It was fun."

Because of her, he acknowledged, and the odd little wrinkle of worry worked its way through his mind again.

Her laughter caused him to smile.

"And different from your highbrow museum benefit. I thought you might like to see how the other half lives."

"I already know," he said wryly.

She laid a hand on his arm. "I'm sorry. I didn't mean to imply—"

"You were teasing," he said, holding her hand trapped between his and his thigh. "No offense taken."

At her place, they walked arm in arm to the door. He opened it with her key, then lifted her into his arms and carried her inside. She snuggled her face into his neck. Her chest pressed into his as she yawned.

"Sometimes I forget what it is to have a good time and not think about business or problems," she said.

"You're too young to be so serious," he scolded, the tenderness she invoked rising in him.

She stroked his cheek. "What about you? You're not so old."

Setting her down by the bed, he began the pleasant

task of undressing her. "There have been times when I've felt I was born old."

"Do you feel that way now?" she asked, her hands busy on his buttons.

"No, not tonight." He ran his palms along her bare sides, down over her hips and thighs, his blood racing at the tactile sensations as they undressed.

He kissed her then and felt her respond. She was life and renewal, an awakening that ran all the way through him.

It wasn't emotion, he assured the part of himself that seemed bent on worrying about it, about them. It was just...great chemistry.

Chapter Eleven

Krista placed potted plants along the window ledge, then settled into her new executive chair. Hard to believe, but it was the middle of May. And Wednesday, the middle of the week. She couldn't wait for Friday.

Be careful, she warned herself. Being with Lance on the weekends was becoming a habit, one she didn't want to learn to depend on. She was trying to live for the moment and whatever joy that brought. She wasn't going to think beyond that.

During the past few weeks, she'd gradually transferred her office to the big one at the end of VIP Row. When Lance was at the plant, they shared the space, spending most of their time in the connecting conference room with managers and engineers coming and going as they worked out changes.

Outside the building, new signs had replaced the old ones. National Home Market, Incorporated, was the official name of the business. The grounds had been spruced up and the old fence enclosing the complex replaced.

There was a flower bed around the old oak tree near where she parked, and picnic tables nearby. With the lovely May weather, many people were using them. She liked that.

These were good changes.

So far, nearly everything had gone well. The retirement offers had gone out a week ago, and several of the eligible employees had accepted, including five of the executive managers. Two positions had been eliminated, and she'd moved the older marketing manager and a couple of assistant managers into the remaining three slots. The younger marketing manager had taken a job at CCS in Denver.

That left one manager to be dealt with. She grimaced, knowing it was time to bite the bullet. After reviewing all the orders over the past two years, she'd compared them to the dollar amounts from past orders. There had been a disturbing decline during that time.

She'd also called some of their former customers

or those whose orders were much smaller than normal. Yesterday, just before closing time, she'd spoken with the executive at the home office of their once steadiest client. He'd been on a business trip to Europe as part of a market expansion, so she'd had to wait a while to finish her investigation.

At the end of the conversation, after he had in strictest confidence confirmed her suspicions, a dismal cloud had settled on her shoulders and stayed.

Now she had to act.

That's why she'd come in at seven that morning. Only she and the security guard were in as yet. She sighed as she reconstructed her research.

Two years ago, their biggest contractor had wanted to buy the company, but Mr. Heymyer wouldn't consider it. Her contact there, the CFO, admitted their offer had been insultingly low.

Then—and this she found hard to believe—Mason had contacted the client and told them the appliance company would go into bankruptcy without their business and they could buy it for a song after that. He'd told other companies that Heymyer couldn't meet their schedules.

Thereafter, Heymyer Appliances began losing orders or having them cut back with increasing frequency.

At seven-thirty, she punched in Lance's speed dial number on the phone. He answered at once.

As usual, her pulse sped up at the sound of his voice. He'd surprised her several times over the past two weeks by arriving at her place during the week, rather than only on the weekend. But he always took a room at the inn across the river when he came for business purposes, too. He was very careful to keep their relationship under wraps.

"I have some bad news and some good news. Which do you want to hear first?" she began.

His chuckle warmed her heart. "The good."

"Okay. We got a new order yesterday from one of our old customers, a special anniversary kitchen set. They loved the idea of the retro fifties styles."

"How big a run?" he asked.

"One hundred thousand three-in-one toaster ovens with coffeemakers and bun warmers, plus a matching number of hand blenders. The brochures of our new product lines and customized features really wowed them."

"So what's the bad news?"

"Mason." She told him what she'd found out. "Three people have verified this. One was the CFO I told you about, and the other are two marketing directors for different clients."

"So what are you going to do?"

She drummed a pencil eraser against the desk while she considered. "He grew up in the plant," she said. "He knows everyone who ever worked here."

"Fire him."

She was silent as she thought of the years she'd known the son and heir of Heymyer Appliances and how engulfed his life had been by company matters, which had always come first with his father. She still felt sorry for Mason.

"If you haven't the stomach for it, then I'll do it," Lance told her, his voice going stern.

Stung that he didn't think she could handle it, she retorted, "No, you won't. *I* will."

"When?"

"As soon as he comes in this morning."

Lance was silent for a moment. "Have a security guard with you."

"I'll call him. I promise," she informed her mentor. "I'll let you know how it comes out."

After she hung up, she stared at the phone as if she might whack it, then she left a message on Mason's voice mail asking him to come to her office when he came in.

She lined up the marketing orders and the canceled contracts, the telephone calls from Mason that showed a lot of traffic between the vice president of Heymyer and certain private numbers at other companies. The pieces all fit.

Mason had wanted to ruin his father. Now, she thought, he wanted revenge on CCS for ruining his plans. The most recent canceled contract had been due to his telling the other company that Heymyer couldn't meet the production schedule due to problems the merger had caused.

She'd been wrong to think him incapable of that kind of betrayal. It called her judgment in question. That was why Lance had been so stern. He was disappointed in her.

When Mason didn't appear an hour after she knew he was in his office, she told Tiff to hold her calls, then she called Mr. Leland, the security guard who had been there for nearly as long as Mason had.

Together they walked into the marketing manager's office through his private door. He was on the phone.

"What the hell?" he said, frowning at them.

"Hang up," she told him. "Now."

"I'll call you back," he said into the phone and slammed it down. "What's happening?" he asked, his manner completely changing as he shifted to his old self, full of casual charm and hubris.

She gestured to the evidence in her hand. "You've been actively undermining the company for the past two years. That's why we lost all these contracts."

"Who says?"

"I do," she said quietly. "I've checked the dates of the orders, the cancellations and the times you called or visited the companies."

He snatched the papers from her and rapidly

scanned through them, then tossed them on the desk. "You can't prove anything with this stuff. It's mere coincidence."

He looked almost gleeful, his smile daring her to do anything. Although she'd never liked him as a friend, still, she'd trusted him.

Aware of a tension headache beating against the back of her skull, she said softly, "Three of the executives I checked with sent written confirmations of their conversations with you. You told them we were having difficulties and could no longer be relied on to meet our obligations."

Mason's face turned red as he cursed at her. "You always do your research, don't you? You think you know everything, but you don't."

His smile was so malicious, she was startled. Mr. Leland moved closer to her.

She gathered the papers. "What did you hope to gain from the sabotage of your own company?"

"Mine? Ha! I've never been more than a flunky here. My father saw to that. You think I didn't have ideas about running the place? No matter. He wouldn't listen to me any more than he did you."

"But if we went bankrupt—"

"Then I was going to be the CEO." His snort of laughter was derisive. "When the new company took over here, I was going to run things. I'd already sold them on my plans."

Krista sucked in a shocked breath. No wonder he'd wanted the company to go down.

"Dear ol' Dad had the last laugh," he continued, fury compressing his face into harsh lines. "He sold the company out from under me. Mom and I were ordered to sign the contract. We had no say in the matter." He looked her over. "You'll learn, just as I did. You'll be out of here as soon as the new owner gets all he wants from you." A sly expression came over his face. "Or has he already gotten everything he wants?"

Krista realized it was time to end the confrontation before things got nasty. "You have one hour to pack your personal items and clear out," she said levelly. "Your final pay will be sent to whatever address you wish."

Mason reached for the phone. "Let's just see if you have the authority to fire anyone." He punched a number on the speed dial pad.

"Mr. Leland," she said to the guard, "would you please escort this gentleman from the building?" Her gaze went to Mason. "If you try to return, you'll be arrested and charged with trespassing."

The guard, who'd watched the son and heir grow to manhood, removed the phone from his hand. He pulled back the chair so Mason could stand. "Let's go," he said in a quiet but authoritative voice.

"Bitch," Mason said, but he was moving toward

the door as he said it. "How long did you sleep with Carrington before you convinced him to buy the place for you?"

That was so absurd, Krista had to suppress a laugh. "As if," she said.

"Did you think you would fool anybody with your pure-as-snow act? His car is at your place every weekend or yours is at the inn where he stays. Everyone here knows what's going on between you."

"Get him out of here," she said to the guard.

Mr. Leland removed the nightstick from his belt. "This way," he ordered.

For several seconds the only sound along VIP Row was that of footsteps going down the stairs and out the front door. When it slammed shut behind the men, she returned to her usual office, not the one at the end of the corridor.

"Here," Tiff said, bringing her a fresh cup of coffee. "Lance called and asked that you call him back when you have time. I, uh, told him what was going on."

"Thanks. I'll do that now."

Lance answered the private line in his office on the first ring. "Tiff said you were with Mason." His voice held a question.

"I fired him and had him escorted out of the building."

"Good. Did he give you any trouble?"

"Not really. I always felt sorry for him, but I

suppose he didn't deserve pity. He betrayed his own father." She told him what Mason had said.

"James got his revenge," Lance murmured thoughtfully. "He sold to me to thwart his son."

"You think he knew about Mason?"

"He was a smart man," was Lance's reply.

"It's hard to believe a family would do that to each other," she said after a beat of silence.

"Believe it," he replied. "So what's your next move?"

She thought of the personnel folders locked in her file cabinet. "Thea. She hasn't done anything about accepting the retirement package. What if she doesn't take it?"

"Give her a strong hint," he said, his manner one of complete confidence in her. "There's one other thing. Can you come up here over the weekend? There's an executive session you need to attend on Monday morning, then we'll head back to Grand Junction that evening."

"Sure. Are there any reports I need to bring?"

"The budget review. You can also announce the news about the latest contract. It'll make us both look good."

"As if you worry about image," she muttered, which drew a chuckle from him. "Is there another benefit to attend?"

"No. I want you to myself," he said in a husky tone.

For how long, she wondered, but it wasn't something she would ever ask. She'd gone into this with her eyes wide open. Seize the moment and all that.

After Mason was gone, the office activity resumed as usual. No one mentioned the former owner or his son. With the change in name as well as ownership, it seemed as if they'd never existed. There was something sad about that.

Her spirits considerably lower than when she'd arrived at work that morning, Krista left the building at six and met Marlyn at the diner. She told her about the difficult day.

"Dealing with people is a lot harder than with machines. I'm much more comfortable with a computer," she concluded the tale. "I've got to go to Denver for a meeting with the CCS executives Monday. Maybe they're going to tell me I'm no longer needed."

"Nah, the raider would do that on his own."

"He isn't a raider. He really is turning the company around and...and making things work."

Marlyn studied her for a long minute. "Have you fallen for him?" she finally asked as the silence stretched like a too tight rubber band between them.

Krista took a drink of soda before answering. "Of course not."

"But you're involved." Her friend sighed. "Don't let him break your heart."

* * *

Due to meetings, Krista hadn't been able to get away from the plant as early as she'd hoped on Friday. She'd switched to the seven o'clock flight and decided to leave her car at the airport, rather than ask someone to drop her off.

Glancing at the dashboard clock, she pushed the accelerator a bit harder. She had to stop by the office for the new budget she'd worked out. She wanted to go over it with Lance and be prepared for any and all questions by the executive committee on Monday.

The whine of a siren alerted her to the vehicle behind her. Red and blue lights flashed at her when she glanced in the rearview mirror.

"Oh, no," she moaned.

Pulling to the side of the road, she retrieved her driver's license and rolled down the window. A cop, who looked around her age, strolled up.

"'Evening," he said. "Could I see your—"

She handed the license over before he could finish.

He studied it, then her. She gave him a tentative smile while she tried to think of something that would excuse her speeding. "Uh, how fast was I going?" she asked.

"A bit over fifty. This is a thirty-five mile speed zone. You in a hurry?"

"Sort of. I'm on my way to the airport, but I forgot some reports at the office. At Heymyer," she added, hoping the name of the company would have some effect. "Uh, National Home Market is its name now."

"Yeah, I read about that in the paper. Hard to believe the old man would sell, isn't it?"

She nodded and wondered if she should just happen to mention she was the head honcho now. She'd never tried to use her influence before. Of course, she'd never had any influence in the past, she recalled wryly.

"I'm going to have to write you up," he said, giving her a sorrowful glance, as if it really pained him to do so.

"You're going to give me a ticket?"

He nodded.

"I've never gotten a ticket before. I've never even been stopped."

"Bummer," he said kindly, but he continued to write on his pad. "We've had a lot of complaints from people in this neighborhood about speeding, so we're patrolling more. You'll need to watch it in the future." He tore off the ticket and handed it to her along with her license.

"Thank you," she said, then realized how ridiculous that sounded.

"Have a nice evening," he called, heading back to the patrol car. "Drive carefully."

"Yeah," she said, rolling up the window.

Very self-conscious about her driving skills, she

pulled back onto the street and, staying a tad below the speed limit, drove to the office. She wondered if the ticket was an omen, a sign that she should slow down and think about where she was going.

Her life had been like a roller coaster since Lance had swept in just over six weeks ago. The days had sped by, and the nights...

Stopping at the entrance to the main building, she dashed to the door, unlocked it, made sure the automatic locking mechanism that had been installed two weeks ago clicked into place, then hurried up the steps.

A light was on in the marketing office.

Her heart started a dull thud of dread. She paused, then went to her office and called the security number.

"Do you know who's in the building?" she asked.

The answer surprised her.

"Uh, you need any help?" the night supervisor asked.

"No, thanks. I just wanted to check before I went barging in," she said lightly.

After a moment of deep breathing for composure, she crossed the hall and went into Mason's office.

"Hello, Thea," she said.

The older woman jerked around from the shredding machine. The noise of the cutting bar stopped when the last sheet went through. The frown of concentration changed into one of ferocity. "What are you doing here?" she demanded.

"I stopped by for some reports. What are you doing?" Krista asked.

The secretary's face slowly developed two bright red spots in her lined cheeks. "Cleaning up some things."

"Why?"

"Mason asked me to. He said he was threatened with arrest if he returned to the property."

She gave Krista a stare so hot with dislike, Krista thought she should have been vaporized on the spot.

The file drawers in the desk were unlocked and two were open. A stack of papers nearly a foot high was on the table beside the shredding machine.

"Tiff and I went through the office Wednesday," Krista said. "Mason's personal items have been sent to him. The rest is company property."

"These are private papers," Thea informed her.

"No," Krista contradicted. "I want them left for the new marketing manager to go through. He'll toss anything he doesn't want."

"Mason asked me—"

"Mason isn't the boss," Krista reminded the secretary. She noticed three answering machine tapes beside the stack of papers. Picking all three up, she read the dates in Thea's neat print. She put the oldest one into the machine and hit the play button.

"Don't," Thea said.

Her tone was almost a snarl and so threatening,

Krista wished she'd brought a guard with her. She merely held up a hand, palm out, in warning.

Thea's voice came from the machine, then Mason's. He asked about the production dates on a contract. The rattle of paper indicated Thea was looking for the information. She gave him the data he wanted.

"Thanks, Thea," Mason said in the most charming voice Krista had ever heard him use. "Six months and I'll be in charge. My father will be history. You and I can run things as we please. And without the CFO."

Krista clicked off the machine and dropped the tapes into her jacket pocket. "I never thought you would betray James. I thought…" Krista gave a brief, ironic laugh. "I thought you were in love with James and that was why you'd stayed all these years."

Thea's lips curled in contempt. "James should have retired years ago. Business was stagnant. If Mason had been CEO, we could have changed things."

"We?" Krista challenged. "What was your role to be in this grand scheme?"

"Executive Director." Her smile gave Krista a chill before she continued, "Your research and financial reports gave Mason the clout he needed. Your ideas were excellent. The other company was going to let us implement them."

"But James caught on and contacted Lance when he realized he couldn't save the company."

"The old fool," Thea muttered. "I did love him

once, but he wouldn't leave his wife. It was her money that saved the place when James took over. He was bold then. His innovations turned things around, and he paid her back."

"Maybe Mason should have married money and bought out his father," Krista suggested dryly.

"I agree," Thea said coldly, but there was a flicker of emotion in her eyes.

Krista wondered when the older woman had switched her loyalty—and her affection?—from the father to the son. She sighed quietly. "As of Monday, you're on vacation. You may come in and collect your things that morning. When you've used up your vacation time, you'll be eligible for the retirement package. Did you look it over?"

"Yes. If I don't retire, you'll have to fire me. I can draw unemployment for months."

"Your employment contract has a mandatory retirement clause," Krista reminded her.

They stared at each other, a silent duel of wills between them. Krista held her ground.

At last Thea looked away. She picked up her purse and a jacket from the executive chair. "You're the one in the boss's…" she deliberately hesitated as she chose the next word, "…pocket now, so you win."

"The keys, please," Krista said. "All of them."

She counted them when Thea laid a key ring on the desk—one to the entrance, another to the CEO suite, one to Mason's door, three smaller ones to various desks.

Thea left without another word.

Krista collected the budget report, called the security supervisor again and told him she and Thea were finished and out of the building for the weekend.

She left her car at the airport and took the flight to Denver. Lance was there when she arrived. She walked past the security monitors and straight into his arms.

"Hey," he said. "Are you okay?"

"Yes." She leaned back and smiled. "Now I am."

His eyes roamed over her face before he nodded. "Let's go home," he murmured, wrapping an arm around her and holding her close as they headed for the car.

Home. A refuge. She felt she needed one at that moment. In his arms, she found it.

Because they were friends. Friends could be safe havens for each other, couldn't they?

Chapter Twelve

Lance woke at dawn. Krista lay on the far edge of the king-size bed, her back to him. He didn't move over and pull her into his arms. It was enough just having her there.

He gazed at the clear sky through the sheer curtains that lined the bank of windows and observed the beginning of the day as the sun came up.

Last night, walking into the penthouse on top of the CCS building, Krista had murmured, "Wow."

It had given him a deep pleasure to bring her into his home. The penthouse had been the last renovation on the building. From an upscale apartment similar to hers, he'd moved in here and found a great deal of satisfaction at having a place of his own.

One that others couldn't take from him or force him to flee in order to hide out.

He stopped the line of thought. That was a long time ago when he'd been young and idealistic.

His gaze went to Krista. After all she'd been through, there was something in her that reminded him of himself as a boy. As a ten-year-old, he'd thought if he tried hard enough he could make things work, that his parents would change, his grandfather would stop hounding them and life would be happy once again.

The hard work part had carried over and was probably the basis of his buying older companies and making them successful once more.

Krista's early experiences had taught her to be wary, but there was still a tender part of her that believed people should work things out and grieved if they didn't, while his lingering lesson had been that people weren't dependable, they didn't change and a person was a fool to believe another's promises.

That didn't mean he couldn't work with other people, but, in a business relationship, if they didn't hold up their end, they were fired or passed over for future contracts.

Krista had been a pleasurable surprise in many ways. She stirred a tenderness in him that was rather unexpected…and maybe a little alarming.

However, he hadn't made a commitment to her. She knew that. She was sharp and savvy. He didn't have to worry about unrealistic expectations.

He relaxed and yawned contentedly, not realizing until that moment how tense he'd become while thinking things through.

Because the nights were still pretty cool even this late in spring, he'd built a fire last night and listened while Krista spoke of betrayal and deceit, the double confrontations—Mason on Wednesday, Thea that evening. And a speeding ticket to top it all, she'd ended ruefully.

Sensing she was emotionally drained, he'd ordered pizza, then had simply held her while they watched TV for the rest of the evening. Reining in the sensual need, he'd tucked her into bed beside him at eleven, their arms and legs entwined, her head snuggled against his shoulder while they shared a pillow.

Surprisingly, he went right to sleep.

At ten after eight, she stirred. "Is it morning?"

"It is," he assured her. "Ready for breakfast?"

"What's on the menu?" The two dimples appeared in her cheeks although the gaze from her big brown eyes was solemn.

"Frozen waffles. Stale cereal. Eggs, maybe."

She groaned and, turning to him, pressed her forehead against his chest. "What do you usually eat?"

"A muffin from the coffee kiosk in the main lobby."

"Let's try the waffles." She patted a yawn and draped an arm and leg over him.

Neither made a move to rise.

"I know what I want," he whispered. "And it isn't food." His body had already made that clear to both of them.

"What is it?" she asked in mock innocence.

"A shower." He tossed the covers back, causing her to squeal as the cool air rushed over them. "This way."

The marble tiles in the bathroom were warm under their bare feet due to the radiant heat. He adjusted the water temperature in the glass-enclosed shower and urged her inside. With soapy hands, he rubbed her all over.

When she gave a little moan and fell against him, his pulse leaped to mach speed. "I can't stand up," she complained.

"Lean on me." He rinsed them off, then turned the spray off and switched to steam.

In a few minutes they were enclosed in a warm mist…and he was sheathed in her warmth as they sat on the built-in bench and made love.

She teased him with her fingers running lightly over him, with the tips of her breasts that brushed him ever so gently, with the alternate tightening and relaxing of her muscles so that he felt caressed all over.

"I want this to last forever," he murmured, stealing

kisses along her throat and collarbone. "But it isn't going to happen," he added with a smile.

"I know."

Krista gazed into Lance's eyes as she returned the smile, then, pressing forward on her knees, she thrust against him, eliciting a harsh gasp.

He stoked her hunger to its highest peak as she moved in the ancient but ever new rhythm.

"Oh, yes," she whispered and buried her face against his neck as the passion rose higher and higher, consuming her with a fire unlike any she'd ever experienced. "Lance. Oh, yes, yes…"

They surged together as one in the final ecstatic spasms of their lovemaking. Then she lay spent and boneless, completely and utterly relaxed. She languidly ran her hands over his back and along his upper arms. His strong fingers massaged a path down her spine. A yawn escaped her.

"If I weren't so hungry, I'd go back to sleep," she told him, sitting up so she could gaze at him. To her, he seemed the perfect specimen of masculinity, strong but gentle in his caresses. His eyes were filled with that indescribable tenderness she was sure she'd seen there before.

When he lifted her by the waist, their bodies moved apart. He rose to his feet, making sure she was steady on hers before releasing her.

She found herself wondering how it would feel to

carry his child, to have it suckle from her breasts and know this special being had been created by them.

But it would never happen. Theirs was a casual relationship with no future, certainly not one that would include something so lasting as children. Sadness filled her heart. Lance would make a wonderful father, one who would never desert his family—

"Breakfast," he reminded her, his gaze gentle on her as he held out his hand while she stepped from the shower.

He turned off the steam while she wrapped a towel around her hair. The fan quickly cleared the mist from the air as they dried off.

The wave that he so carefully tried to comb smooth fell over his forehead and ended in a curl. She slipped her hand under it and felt the damp strand wrap around her finger...the way he had sneaked inside and wrapped around her heart.

Dressed in jeans, T-shirt and her jogging shoes, Krista sat at the breakfast bar and sipped fresh-brewed coffee while Lance toasted waffles.

She gazed at the mountains, her thoughts troubled by the revelation of twenty minutes past. Swallowing hard, she admitted she'd done a foolish thing, that somehow she'd let him get past her defenses. How and when had this happened?

"The view is great, isn't it?" he asked, his eyes following hers, then returning to her face when she smiled and nodded. He placed the two plates on the table and passed her the syrup in a crystal pitcher.

"Fancy," she said, pouring some over the waffle.

"I'm trying to impress you. When I'm alone, I pour straight from the bottle."

She laughed. "I suspected as much. So do I."

With her fork, she gestured around the combined living area, which was decorated in blue and burgundy wallpaper and drapes, offset with creamy white woodwork and lots of honey beige on the upper part of the walls. There were many windows along the walls and French doors to the rooftop patio.

"Did you have a professional choose your colors and furniture?" she asked.

"Yes. There's a decorator in the building. I thought it made sense to use someone who leased from me." He paused. "Jenna helped with the colors."

"I see," she said levelly.

"I've known her since her grandfather came on the board of CCS about seven years ago. It was something she wanted to do and I didn't have any preferences," he continued. "Other than friendship, there's never been anything between us."

"You don't have to explain," she quickly said. "Your home is very attractive."

"I picked out the bed," he told her with a wicked grin. "I wanted it big and very comfortable."

"Well, you succeeded in that."

"I've only been in the penthouse about a year. It was the last thing to be renovated. Actually, you're my first overnight guest," he added softly, his eyes lambent with the memory of shared passion. "My only solitary guest."

Heat seeped into her cheeks as relief spread through her. She was jealous, she realized. She hadn't wanted Jenna or any other woman to be here with him, not in any intimate sense. "Good," she said firmly.

He gave her an understanding perusal. "I sometimes have to fight the urge to snatch you away from Toby when you two are deep into some problem."

"You don't," she said, not believing it for a second, even though she wanted to.

"I do." He leaned across the table and planted a firm kiss on her mouth. "It's more difficult than I thought to keep the personal out of the business side of our lives. I have to be on guard that I don't touch you or act familiar. Especially when I want to kiss the blazes out of you while you're giving a report during a staff meeting."

She laughed and the little storm of jealousy passed in a tidal wave of joy. "What shall we do today?"

"I thought we would take in the sights, then stop for lunch at one of my favorite hamburger places."

"Ah, the battle for first place between my favorite and yours. Five bucks says the Doggy Diner is the best."

"You're on."

Twenty minutes later, as they prepared to leave the building, his cell phone rang. She knew the news wasn't good as a frown appeared on his handsome face.

"Yes," he said. "I'll meet them at the hospital."

When he hung up, he gazed at her in silence for a couple of seconds.

"That was Morgan," he said. "The ambulance just picked up my grandfather. He's having trouble breathing. I need to head for the hospital. You can stay here, if you like, or you can come with me."

"I'll go with you."

"It might be a long wait," he warned.

"That doesn't matter. We'll stay however long it takes. That's what friends do for each other."

He gave her a hard look, then took her hand and led the way to the parking garage. In less than five minutes, they were on their way to the hospital on the western side of town.

Krista went into a small waiting room in the cardiac wing of the hospital while Lance continued down the corridor to his grandfather's room.

The doctor had reported Mr. Carrington was "stable," but he was having difficulty breathing due to pneumonia. They had added medication to his IV and he was resting.

She recalled how dry and papery his skin had felt when they met. While the older man appeared strong and solid, there was the frailty of age about him, too.

After fifteen minutes, Lance came to the door. "Would you like to come to the room? We can sit there as well as in here. I sent Morgan home to get some rest. He was up most of the night, but Grandfather wouldn't let him call an ambulance. When he passed out, Morgan called anyway."

"Your grandfather is lucky to have someone like Morgan and his wife to help him."

"That's what they're paid to do."

"I think they go beyond paid staff," she said softly. "They seem loyal. And truly concerned for him."

Lance shrugged as they walked along the hall. "They loved my grandmother. She hired Morgan as a gardener when her pastor asked for help for them. Morgan and Carly were a homeless young couple with a child to raise. The two women loved cooking and gardening. They became friends as well as employer and employee when Carly took over the kitchen after the old chef retired."

Krista smiled. "I can't imagine having a chef. At our house, the kids had to plan and prepare a meal one night a week. When we complained because my brother had the same thing each time and I reminded him we needed green vegetables, he switched our chips and baked beans to broccoli and lime Jell-O to go with the hamburgers."

When Lance chuckled, she did, too.

After using the alcohol wash on their hands, they entered the room. She was shocked at how pale and drawn his grandfather looked. Tubes of oxygen were clipped to his nose while an IV dripped into a vein on the back of his hand.

"There's coffee at the nurse's station," Lance told her. "I'm going to have a cup. Do you want one?"

"Please," she replied softly.

When he returned, he brought the cups and the local newspaper. They read sections of it for the rest of the morning. His grandfather slept as if exhausted until the lunch tray came.

"I don't want anything to eat," he told the young girl who woke him.

"You might change your mind," she said cheerfully, putting the tray on the server and wheeling it to the bed, then raising the bed so he could sit up. She swung the server arm across him.

Lance went to the bedside after the aide left. "Can I help you with anything?"

His grandfather's eyes, so like Lance's, flicked from Lance to Krista. The older man smiled. "So. You're back."

She stood and went to the other side of the bed. "Yes. We have a meeting Monday morning."

"But you came up for the weekend," he concluded.

"I'm showing her the town," Lance said dryly.

His body might be frail, Krista thought, but his mind wasn't. There was speculation in the silvery depths of that keen gaze as he studied her, then his grandson.

"That's nice," he said. Lifting his hands, he frowned at the IV attachment, then removed the paper covering on a glass of tea that had two chips of ice left in it. "Help me get the covers off," he said to Lance, his tone once more querulous, as if he resented being where he was.

And he probably did, Krista mused as she propped a hip on the wide window ledge and stared out at the city and the hilly landscape.

Closing her eyes for a few seconds, she felt a sense of renewal in her life and knew it came from her feelings for Lance.

Locking her fingers tightly in her lap to stop the tremor that rushed over her, she tried to look on the bright side. In four and a half months, she would be free to leave and Lance would never know how foolish she'd been to fall in love with him.

Krista glanced up from the magazine she was reading when Mr. Carrington began mumbling in his sleep. Several times during the afternoon, his dreams, or maybe his conscience, had troubled him.

Lance had gone to the waiting room to take a call on his cell phone. The manager at one of his other companies had needed some help with a problem.

"Lance," his grandfather said in a sad voice, then, "young fool," he muttered in a stern tone.

She laid the magazine aside as Mr. Carrington moved one hand in a restless gesture. Worried that he might disturb the IV, she went to him. Taking his hand, she held it between both of hers to warm the icy cold flesh.

Staring at his ashen face and sunken cheeks, she found herself praying that he wouldn't die, that he and Lance would find their way to understanding or forgiveness or whatever they needed for peace between them. Families needed each other.

"What is it?" a deep voice said behind her.

She felt Lance's warmth along her back as he came close. She smiled over her shoulder at him. "Your grandfather seems restless. He's been talking in his sleep for the past few minutes. I was afraid he would dislodge the IV needle."

He glanced at the old man's hand in hers. "I'll take over. Why don't you walk around or go to the cafeteria, if you like? We never did get that hamburger."

She moved aside and let him take her place beside the bed. His grandfather rolled his head from side to side, his lips moving, a frown furrowing his forehead.

"Lindy-girl," he said.

"My grandmother," Lance explained. "Her name was Linda. He used to call her Lindy-girl when he teased her."

A picture of the old man as a young and dashing one, dynamic and charming like his grandson, came to her.

Pity clogged her throat, and she had to swallow hard before answering. "I think I might get something to eat. Would you like anything?"

"They make a good beef stew. If they have any, I'll take a bowl of that and a couple of cartons of milk." He reached for his wallet.

"I'll get it," she volunteered. "My boss pays well."

That drew a smile from him and wiped some of the worry off his face.

Downstairs, she followed the signs to the cafeteria and found it pretty busy. The wall clock indicated the time was one-thirty. No wonder she was hungry.

Getting a tray, she loaded it with two bowls of the stew, a bunch of crackers, one large bowl of fruit, a slice of chocolate cake and three cartons of low fat milk.

Tray in hand, she paused outside Mr. Carrington's room. The door was closed, but not quite latched.

She heard Lance's voice, then his grandfather's.

Thinking Lance might be helping the older man with some private business, she set the tray on a nearby stool and rolled it close to the door, then waited until she got an all-clear signal.

Down the hall, a gurney pushed through double

swinging doors leading into the cardiac surgical unit. A draft of air swirled around Krista as the doors swung closed.

"How old is Krista?" she heard Mr. Carrington ask.

Glancing at the room's door, she saw it was ajar. She wondered if she could close it without the men noticing.

"Twenty-five," Lance answered.

"She's pretty."

"She's also a whiz at finances." He laughed softly. "She and Toby are like two sides of the same coin when they get together and start crunching numbers."

"That's...good."

She heard the wheezy quality of Mr. Carrington's breathing and thought he sounded worse. Her worry deepened.

"Yes. She's an asset to the company."

"And you?"

"What about me?" Lance asked, his voice changing from humorous to hard-edged.

"She's staying with you, isn't she?" the older man asked. "Isn't that why she came here with you?"

"She's my guest."

"At your place?" Mr. Carrington persisted in spite of his grandson's repressive tone.

"Yes."

"Are you going to marry her?"

Krista felt as if all the blood drained right out of her head as she waited for Lance's answer.

"No," was the blunt reply.

"Foolish," his grandfather reprimanded. "She'd be good in business and at home. Everyone, even you, needs someone in his life. People need connection. It's what keeps us human. A wife can bring a man great happiness."

"I don't want a wife," Lance said in a dead-level manner. "I don't need anyone to supply me with happiness. I have everything I want."

"My fault...broke that boy's heart," the older man mumbled, apparently lapsing into the past. "I could have helped, but I was too stubborn. Your mother—"

"Don't talk about my mother," Lance said in a snarl.

Krista couldn't get her lungs to function. Her breath locked behind a knot in her throat as sorrow for both men rushed over her. The tears pressed insistently against her control. She glanced around desperately. She needed to get away, to be alone.

The waiting room...

Before she could act, the door swung inward. Lance stood on the other side. She composed her face to stillness.

"Krista," he said in a low tone that sounded utterly weary. "I'm sorry—"

"I, uh, I brought lunch," she interrupted.

"What I said in there," he continued, tilting his head toward the sick room, "has nothing to do with us."

"I know." She waved his explanation aside. "You

don't have to explain. I don't expect anything from you or our relationship, uh, outside business and, and…" She couldn't think of a polite word for the wildly passionate moments they shared.

She was aware of the flush of heat radiating from her entire body, that terrible vat of humiliation she'd felt once before in her life and had tried to guard against ever since. Only it was worse this time.

He touched her hot cheek. "I didn't mean to embarrass you," he said softly.

"It doesn't matter." She took his hand and met his concerned gaze. "I think you and your grandfather should talk. He's worried about you, about your past and his part in it. He needs your forgiveness."

A muscle tensed in Lance's jaw. "The past is over," he said in the harshest voice she'd ever heard from him.

She shook her head. "It's never over until we can get over it. I know how it feels to be taken from those you love, whether by an accident or…or because of their own shortcomings."

"This doesn't concern you," he said, a warning.

"I know. But your grandfather is right. Everyone needs others in order to find happiness. Humans are social animals. We really can't make it alone and without…without love."

He tried to pull away.

She held on to his hand. "I think, before you can accept that, you need to forgive your grandfather for not helping your parents. And maybe you need to forgive *them* for being unable to give up the bad things in their lives for the one perfect, good thing— their child."

He cursed, so low she almost didn't hear him, and removed his hand from her grasp.

"And most of all, you need to forgive that ten-year-old who couldn't make the world right no matter how hard he tried, no matter how much he loved," she finished softly.

"You should listen to her, son," his grandfather called out hoarsely.

Lance stepped into the hall, pulling the door closed behind him. "Being lovers doesn't give you the right to barge into the rest of my life."

"I know, but you're making a mistake," she said, determined to make him listen, "and you're too smart not to know it. You wanted help for your mother, but unless she was willing to accept it, you couldn't force it on her. She made choices, too, bad choices—"

He leaned forward, his glare direct and unforgiving. "You weren't there. You don't know anything about her, or what she went through. She tried, but she couldn't do it on her own, not while my father was alive."

"Or later when she was alone," Krista added sadly.

He stared at her, his eyes guarded, devoid of the

tenderness she'd come to expect. She'd overstepped the boundaries between them, a thing he wouldn't allow.

Krista pressed her hands against the cool, green wall for support as he turned and walked down the hall, then out of sight.

Chapter Thirteen

Krista grabbed her suitcase from the backseat and dashed through the drizzle that obscured the surrounding lawn. The lights along the sidewalk were halos of safety in the storm and the night.

Snug in her apartment, she put on warm pajamas and fleece-lined slippers, then made a cup of hot cocoa and settled in her favorite chair.

The wind made piping sounds as it rounded the corner of the building and blew against the chimney. She'd never felt so totally alone in her life.

After waiting until Lance returned to the hospital, she'd taken a taxi to the inn and left a message on the private line at his penthouse, asking that her suitcase be sent over before Monday so she could prepare for the meeting with the CCS executive committee.

A cab had brought the luggage and Toby had picked her up on Monday morning. "I don't know what happened," he'd said to her, "but I think Lance hurt you. Don't judge him too harshly."

"Well, I barged in where angels fear to tread and all that," she'd replied on a light note. "He told me to barge right back out."

Toby had studied her while stopped for a red light, then sighed. "He's a fool if he lets you go."

"It isn't like that. We both knew the rules."

"I think it is like that," Toby had said with his own brand of stubbornness.

Placing the steaming cup on the side table, Krista laid her head against the comfortable padding as she reviewed the past ten days. At the Monday meeting, she'd been stunned when Lance announced she was now the CEO of the appliance company. The executive officers had stood and applauded while her thoughts scattered like mice caught in the pantry by the resident cat.

During the rest of the week, after she returned to Grand Junction, her dealings with Lance had been brief and aloof while those with Toby had been long and complicated.

To Tiff's delight, Krista had promoted the secretary

to executive assistant and told her to clear the many file cabinets and store the accumulated folders of the past three years. The remainder were to be destroyed. Tiff had set to work on Thea's closely guarded domain with glee. Thea's retirement papers had been received by the personnel office on Wednesday.

On Friday, Krista had driven to Idaho and spent Memorial Day weekend with her family. She'd let them think her long silences were due to the added responsibility of being in charge of a company at her tender age.

Well, there was that, but she was proud of the promotion and the accomplishment it represented.

On the other hand, she felt bruised and foolish for falling in love. However, she wasn't ready to talk about it, not even to her beloved family, all of whom had been home.

Her brother and his wife had announced they were expecting a baby in the winter. She'd been happy for them and thrilled at the prospect of being an aunt.

A giant surge of the love she had for all her family flooded her heart. She wasn't like Lance. She couldn't lock her feelings away from what was happening in her life. She still wanted everyone to be safe and happy.

There was one bright note on the relationship front—Marlyn had reported she and Linc were going to counseling to see if they could sort out their marital problems. That was very good news.

The wind gusted against the building, rattling the patio furniture as if impatient to get inside. The keening notes of its passage sounded lonely to her.

She wondered if Lance was at home or his grandfather's place. Toby had reported the older man was at home once more, convalescing from the illness. Lance had stayed at the lovely estate all week. Perhaps the two men, who were so much alike in height and looks, had reached an understanding that each could live with.

It was none of her business, at any rate. If she concentrated hard enough, she could forget Lance for minutes at a time.

Lance sat in the library, a room that he was, oddly, at ease in nowadays. The rain beat against the dark windowpane in an impatient drumming, as if demanding to be admitted into the warm, comfortable room.

His grandfather had nodded off after dinner. The old man had been alarmingly quiet after coming home from the hospital. Lance had expected repeated attempts to tell him what to do with his life and remind him of all the mistakes he was making in it.

Such as Krista.

Okay, he missed her. He admitted it. Returning to the penthouse and finding her gone had bothered him. Her message that she was safe at the inn hadn't assuaged the feeling. Seeing her on Monday had been a relief.

At the meeting, she'd been composed, albeit a bit stunned at being named the CEO. She'd handled the news very well, smiling and gracious as she thanked them and promised to do her best.

As if she could do less.

He couldn't help the smile that tugged at his mouth or the tender feeling that invaded his consciousness. That was the way she affected him—

"Son?"

Lance glanced at his grandfather, who now sat up in the recliner and gazed at him. "Ah, you're awake. Are you ready to finish the game of gin rummy?"

"You just want to play because you're close to winning," the old man grumbled good-naturedly.

Lance laughed. "Right."

"Have you heard from Krista?"

Lance tensed at the direct question. "No, but I'm sure she's fine."

The wind filled the silence with a low moan around the eaves that was disturbing. It seemed…forlorn.

"I hurt her," his grandfather continued in a regretful tone. "I shouldn't have brought up the subject of marriage when she was there."

"We both hurt her," Lance said.

The truth of that filtered through any defense he could erect. Krista, with her concern for others, had cared about them, two stubborn men who had never been able to meet halfway although, God knows, his grandmother had tried.

Krista, with her wariness about involvement, had let him into her personal life and her arms.

And her heart?

He knew the answer, had known it that day when he'd lashed out at her and walked away. She'd stayed at the hospital with his grandfather until he returned, then she'd left. He'd given her the code to unlock the penthouse door, but she hadn't gone near the place.

Perhaps that was the reason he stayed on here. One night with her, and his home had suddenly become too lonely to endure.

He cursed silently, but it didn't hold back the guilt, or the longing. Yeah, he missed her.

"What can we do about it?" his grandfather asked.

Lance stared out the window. With the storm and the night, it reflected the room and the two men who sat there in the lamplight, each filled with thoughts they found difficult to share.

"She said I needed to forgive my parents," he murmured.

"Brandon wasn't the best of fathers. He didn't have a good example. I demanded too much from him…as I did from you."

"It doesn't matter," Lance told him. "You took me in and gave me a home. I didn't appreciate that fact. Until recently."

His grandfather sighed. "Your father retreated into alcohol. You locked your feelings away so that no one could get too close. Except maybe this time, someone did."

Lance stiffened, but he knew what was coming.

"Krista got to you. I think she loves you. If you're lucky, maybe she still does."

"Even though I walked away from her, cutting her off as if she was nothing to me? The way I've always done with you when things got too deep," he added.

Inside, he felt a withering of old resentments and a softening, like the earth thawing in the warmth of spring after a terribly long winter. Something new and painful, something that had waited a long time, wanting to grow and blossom in the summer sun beat at him.

"It doesn't matter about me, but it does about her," his grandfather said quietly. "If you love her, tell her. She needs to know it, but most importantly, you need to know it, too. And you need to let yourself accept her love."

Lance stared at his grandfather for a long minute. To open himself up, even to Krista, could be dangerous. It meant being vulnerable again.

"Don't be a damn coward," the old man growled at him.

Lance returned the unexpected glare, able to give just as good as he got from the old tyrant.

"You think I don't know how you feel?" his grandfather demanded. "When my son died, when my wife was near death, I could have shared my grief with you, but I closed myself off, the way you do when you're hurt…both of us, too damn afraid to reach out for the good things."

His voice trailed off as he shook his head, his face grim with equal parts despair and disgust.

Lance fought the desire to walk out and ignore the truth that beat at him, to push the pain in his chest back into the cold storage locker that had guarded his heart for so long. He sensed a moment had arrived in his life that couldn't be ignored.

In front of him was a line. To step over it was to seek the future, to go to Krista and risk being hurt.

Hurt? Yes, because…because he loved her, had done so almost from the moment they'd met.

"Your father loved you," his grandfather said after a few minutes. "Never doubt that. But it was your mother who tried the hardest to be there for you. I know now that she represented the happiness and security a child needs. It was her love that gave you the perseverance to face life on your own terms, not anything that I said or did. I didn't understand. I took you away—"

"I couldn't have saved her," Lance broke in. "I always thought I could. If she'd been given just one more chance, if I could have been with her, I thought everything would have been different. But it wasn't to be."

His grandfather breathed a long, sad sigh. "No, it wasn't to be. We all wasted our chances to make amends—me, your father, your mother. It could be different for you, if you act before it's too late."

Gray eyes, so like his own, stared at him, compelling him to see the truth as the older man saw it.

"You can save yourself from a future filled with regret," his grandfather told him. "Don't throw away a chance at the greatest happiness a man can know, that of a wife and family who love him. Maybe I didn't listen to your grandmother when I should have, but there was never a time when I didn't know she was the very center of my heart."

A hot ache formed behind Lance's eyes. He paced the room and tried to will it away, but it refused to budge.

He thought of the past, of his mother's tears. *I love you. Be a good boy.*

He'd tried to be worthy of her love for him, to live a decent life, knowing that's what she wanted for him. He'd tried to succeed where his father had failed. He'd tried…but it had taken a toll, he realized.

Everything he'd done had been rooted in the past while he'd locked his heart away. But now…now his heart refused to be shoved into that cold, safe but lonely place any longer.

"Krista," he muttered.

"Ah, you finally woke up," the old man said gruffly. "It's about damn time."

Krista replaced the phone and rocked back in the big executive chair. A new financial officer would be coming in next week, one she'd chosen and the CCS board had approved.

As they'd approved all the changes she and Toby had come up with.

In the outer office, her name was on the door as the CEO. Tiff was ecstatic at the changes. Krista had to admit there was an air of purpose in the company now. It was lean and mean at seven hundred and five employees. The older employees liked taking new ones under their collective wing and teaching them the ropes of cross-training and team work.

Yet despite her ongoing success, she still experienced the familiar pang of longing.

Get over it, she advised herself.

She knew firsthand that people could get over a lot of things in life…not that they didn't hurt, but a person survived. So did a heart.

Yeah, well, it got tiresome, holding all the cracks together with the flimsy tape of willpower while waiting for time to do its healing trick.

She managed a smile. Being sardonic helped. Working helped even more. She'd come in at six that morning so she could talk to the incoming CFO back in New Jersey before he reported in for his final week with his present company.

Other than security, no one was about. She could nap for an hour, then she wanted to go over the agenda for the staff meeting before they met at nine—

Footsteps in the hallway jarred her out of sleep mode. She listened as they approached her end of the corridor.

It was probably the guard making his rounds.

The outer door opened and closed. A tall figure appeared at the frosted glass. The door opened, and Lance entered.

He closed the door, then stood there, his hands in his pockets as those wintry gray eyes roamed over her face.

At a disadvantage lounging in the big chair, she rose and looked him over, too. "Were we expecting you?" she finally asked when it became clear he wasn't going to lead the conversation. "Or are you here for the staff meeting?"

It wasn't like him to just show up, though. Her heart began beating in a slow, hard tempo, causing vibrations through her entire body.

He shook his head. "I'm here for you," he said, his voice low and filled with nuances she didn't understand.

Her lungs constricted, but she knew she had to

maintain her composure at all costs. Big business tycoons didn't throw themselves into another tycoon's arms, now did they?

She pressed her fingertips on the desk and smiled at him with all the confidence at her command while she searched for something to say. "Did you drive over from Denver this morning?"

"Yes."

"Oh. Uh, would you like a cup of coffee? There're muffins, too, if you're hungry."

"I am," he stated flatly.

He walked around the desk and stood a mere six inches from her. She fought the urge to back away. She knew a challenge when she saw one, and looking into his eyes, she thought they were about to have a showdown.

Over what, she hadn't a clue.

He touched her cheek, just the barest brush of his fingertips. It sent a lightning strike through her, making her knees weak and cracking the composed facade. She stepped away from his touch, even as she longed to lean into him.

"Hungry for you," he continued, his voice going very soft. "For what we shared. For what we could have in the future, if we both really, really try."

Her heart lit up like a Fourth of July fireworks display, but she quickly put a damper on her foolish thoughts. She knew not to let longing override common sense. A person had to be practical, hard-nosed and logical in the business world, not sentimental.

"No. It was a mistake to become personally involved. It makes things too complicated." She managed a croaky laugh and added, "For me, if not for you. Sorry about that."

Her voice had gone all husky and tight on her. It also held a note of desperation as visions of the future he described bloomed in her mind. That future sounded really, really enticing. And in the end, it would really, really break her heart. She sighed in despair.

He shook his head, negating her words. "You're the bravest person I know. You can handle anything. If you're willing to start over, I'll try to be like that, too."

While she understood the meaning of each individual word, together they made no sense to her. "If you're trying to confuse me, you've succeeded. If you want to continue an affair, I—I don't..." She had to pause and take a calming breath.

"No," he said quickly, moving closer, crowding her space. "Actually, I'm thinking of a merger, a lifelong one, complete with children, if that's what you want, and a home where we can all be together as a family, like in the house up on the river."

Lance smiled as he gazed into bewildered eyes that reminded him of rich brown velvet.

He pulled her into his arms. "Could you take a lifetime with me? Would you?"

She was silent so long, he felt as if needles were being stuck into his heart. Then two little dimples winked into being.

"You mean it," she whispered, cupping her hands around his face, touching him tenderly, sweetly, lovingly. "You really mean it."

"With all my heart," he vowed. "And that's the hardest thing I've admitted in a long time."

She hugged him close, unable to hold the words in. "I love you."

He nodded. "All the way here, I kept worrying about that. I decided you had to love me because I couldn't bear to think otherwise. It was too painful." He rubbed his hands up and down her back, absorbing her warmth into his being. "My grandfather was positive you felt the same way I did—"

"Your grandfather?"

Lance's smile was wry. "He and I are on solid ground for once. We totally agree where you're concerned. We both want you in the family. He said he might marry you himself if I didn't get on with it."

Krista couldn't keep from laughing even as she ran her hands into Lance's smooth dark hair. The stubborn wave fell over his forehead in a tousled manner she found endearing. "I'd rather marry you," she said softly. "A merger sounds just right. If that's what you're offering."

"It is. I do love you," he said, leaning close to

her ear. "I'll try to be the husband you want, the one you deserve."

"You already are."

They moved at the same moment and their lips met in a kiss, one of promise that Krista knew would never be broken.

When he sat in the big, comfortable chair, she just naturally fit into his lap. A long time later, she heard voices in the conference room.

"I forgot about the staff meeting!"

His smile melted her insides as he touched the frown lines between her eyes. "How long does it last?"

"About two hours. Are you attending?"

"No. I have some calls to make." He set her on her feet. "You can handle it."

They smiled at each other.

"I can't believe I'm not dreaming," she told him as she gathered her papers and placed the agenda sheet on top.

"It's no dream." He kissed her lightly. He kissed her deeply, lovingly.

It was a perfect meeting of hopes and dreams.

* * * * *

New York Times *bestselling author*
Linda Lael Miller
is back with a new romance
featuring the heartwarming
McKettrick family
from Silhouette Special Edition.

SIERRA'S HOMECOMING
by Linda Lael Miller

On sale December 2006,
wherever books are sold.

Turn the page for a sneak preview!

Soft, smoky music poured into the room.

The next thing she knew, Sierra was in Travis's arms, close against that chest she'd admired earlier, and they were slow dancing.

Why didn't she pull away?

"Relax," he said. His breath was warm in her hair.

She giggled, more nervous than amused. What was the matter with her? She was attracted to Travis, had been from the first, and he was clearly attracted to her. They were both adults. Why not enjoy a little slow dancing in a ranch-house kitchen?

Because slow dancing led to other things. She took

a step back and felt the counter flush against her lower back. Travis naturally came with her, since they were holding hands and he had one arm around her waist.

Simple physics.

Then he kissed her.

Physics again—this time, not so simple.

"Yikes," she said, when their mouths parted.

He grinned. "Nobody's ever said that after I kissed them."

She felt the heat and substance of his body pressed against hers. "It's going to happen, isn't it?" she heard herself whisper.

"Yep," Travis answered.

"But not tonight," Sierra said on a sigh.

"Probably not," Travis agreed.

"When, then?"

He chuckled, gave her a slow, nibbling kiss. "Tomorrow morning," he said. "After you drop Liam off at school."

"Isn't that…a little…soon?"

"Not soon enough," Travis answered, his voice husky. "Not nearly soon enough."

nocturne™

**Explore the dark and sensual
new realm of paranormal romance.**

HAUNTED
BY LISA CHILDS

**The first book in the riveting
new 3-book miniseries, Witch Hunt.**

DEATH CALLS
BY CARIDAD PIÑEIRO

**Darkness calls to humans,
as well as vampires...**

*On sale December 2006,
wherever books are sold.*

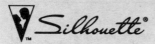

REQUEST YOUR FREE BOOKS!

2 FREE NOVELS PLUS 2 FREE GIFTS!

SPECIAL EDITION™

Life, Love and Family!

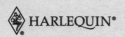

HARLEQUIN®

American ROMANCE®

IS PROUD TO PRESENT

COWBOY VET
by Pamela Britton

Jessie Monroe is the last person on earth
Rand Sheppard wants to rely on, but he needs
a veterinary technician—yesterday—and she's the
only one for hire. It turns out the woman who
destroyed his cousin's life isn't who Rand thought
she was. And now she's all he can think about!

"Pamela Britton writes the kind of
wonderfully romantic, sexy, witty romance
that readers dream of discovering
when they go into a bookstore."

—*New York Times* bestselling author
Jayne Ann Krentz

Cowboy Vet *is available from*
Harlequin American Romance in December 2006.

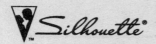

COMING NEXT MONTH

SSECNM1106

SPECIAL EDITION